Gods Wait To Punish

&

Other Selected Short Stories

Gods Wait To Punish

&

Other Selected Short Stories

Sivasankari

Translator
Subha Pande

First Edition: 2023

Gods Wait To Punish

Sivasankari

ISBN: 978-93-94922-38-9

Pustaka Digital Media Pvt. Ltd.
#7-002, Mantri Residency,
Bannerghatta Main Road, Bengaluru - 560 076
Karnataka, India
+91 7418555884

Contents

About The Book

These short stories by iconic Tamil writer Sivasankari, published over the years in reputed Tamil magazines have captured the readers' minds for decades. She is a keen observer of society and her stories bring out the social ills that plague our society. Her stories reflect the times and act as a mirror for the readers. She covers a wide range of issues like domestic violence, sexual abuse, child abuse, misogyny, patriarchy, problems faced by the aged and so on.

These include stories on the challenges faced during the Corona epidemic as well.

This compilation consists of seventeen selected stories written between 1974 and 2021. These are timeless tales that raise issues that are relevant and prevalent in our society even today. They are thought provoking and have evoked tremendous response from the readers over the years. Though written originally in Tamil, we are certain that they have a global appeal and resonate with readers across age groups, geography, and gender.

Pustaka

Gods wait to punish

"Then? What happened?"

Bhaskaran Nair's eyes opened wide and he blurted out the question.

Paramaguru bent down and tapped his cigarette on the ashtray. He had been drinking for the past hour or so and his face was flushed and glowed with narcissistic pride.

He said arrogantly,

"What do you think happened? The next two days were like a dream! She is known to be a hot headed woman… doesn't fall even for millionaires! But she followed me like a puppy. All my friends were stunned… Those were truly exciting days, Bhaskaran…"

The Major stopped speaking and watched with pride the agitation he had created in the men present there.

Nair had gone cold, while Seth, Ravi, and Daniel sat by the bonfire with drinks that they had forgotten to have… the Major enjoyed the sight!

"You all are stunned listening to this; what would you say if you heard what happened in Jammu… I am sure you won't believe it…" The Major guffawed aloud and narrated the experience.

What a lucky man! He has enjoyed every moment of his adventurous life!

Major Paramaguru narrating his interesting stories to his envious friends was not a recent development. This has been happening for the past four years. That was when Major Paramaguru had quit the army and settled down in his home town Yercaud.

The Major's magnificent bungalow was on the road leading from the lake to the town. It was just a stone's throw away from Hotel Chevroy's. His bungalow was surrounded by vast, green lawns and was hidden by a thick wood full of tall Eucalyptus trees. The lawn had colorful flower beds around it with a variety of enchanting blooms.

Paramaguru's father, Sambandam, owned a big coffee plantation in Yercaud. Paramaguru was his only child and Sambandam hoped that his son would take over the plantation after his studies, but the son had other plans. Paramaguru had aspired to join the army ever since his childhood, and he did exactly that.

"Why do you need to join the army? Listen to me, son. We have enough money for three generations. Why do you have to work elsewhere? I am really worried for you my son…" His mother's pleading and emotional letters had no effect whatsoever on Paramaguru, and his parents decided to let their son do as he pleases.

They put their plan into action when their son came home on leave a couple of years later.

"Guru, you know that Appa has cardiac problems. He wishes that you get married soon. Please listen to us, son." For some reason Paramaguru paid heed to his mother's fervent appeal and consented to get married.

Soon enough, Paramguru's parents got him married to the beautiful, well mannered, and obedient girl, Soundaram. Sambandam was really happy because he was certain that his son's military career wouldn't last long because of his marriage. But he was wrong.

Soundaram was indeed very beautiful. Everyone thought she looked like a goddess in her Kanjeevaram silk saree, big bindi on her forehead and hair decked in flowers; but Paramaguru did not think so. He found her too traditional and was not happy with her dressing sense. Anyway, Guru didn't bother much because he was confident that he would be able to change her once she moved to the army cantonment with him.

They left for Dehradun once his two month leave got over and set up their home. Paramaguru tried hard for six months to change Soundaram and get her used to army life but he failed miserably. She refused to speak to the army officers who visited their place. She never accompanied him for parties hosted by his colleagues. If Paramaguru forced her she declined saying, "I don't like the way the male officers get cozy with women and touch them while having a conversation. I can't take the loud laughter... the drinking..."

Paramaguru soon realized that it would be difficult to convince her or change her and decided to send her back to Yercaud.

"This place doesn't suit her... Let her be in Yercaud, I will take a transfer and join you as soon as possible." He assured his parents, left Soundaram with them, and returned to Dehradun.

"What happened to your transfer Guru?"

Whenever his father asked him either in person or in his letters, Paramaguru would conveniently find excuses like, "I have got posted to a border post, it will take time."

Or

"I am in training and can't do anything for some time."

However Paramaguru made it a point to come home on leave for ten days every year like a dutiful son and husband and go back.

A few years passed like this and once when he came home on leave, Soundaram conceived and as luck would have it, Paramaguru got a promotion as soon as his daughter was born. The moment he laid his eyes on his beautiful ten day old baby and kissed her forehead, he felt a strange tug in his heart and a wave of affection rose within him. His parents named her Lakshmi. Since she looked like an adorable doll, Paramaguru called her Dolly.

Paramaguru was tempted to take his darling daughter and his wife with him but seeing that Soundaram hadn't changed one bit and was as rustic and unpolished as before, he changed his mind.

In any case, with his impressive personality and intelligence, he never faced a dearth of female companions wherever he was posted-be it Pune, Dehradun, or Ladakh. He didn't miss his family at all.

When Dolly was six years old, Soundaram fell in the bathroom and suffered a severe brain hemorrhage and her condition turned serious. Paramaguru rushed home hearing the news.

Soundaram, who was in her last moments, and had never spoken to him eye to eye, held his hands to her heart and said, "As you sow… so shall you… reap… Our deeds-good… and bad, … will affect our child… too. Beware… The mills of… God grind… slow but sure… Remember that!" She wanted to say a lot more, but ended up saying those words incoherently and breathed her last.

Sow, reap, God… what was she trying to say? Paramaguru couldn't understand anything but he just nodded his head for her satisfaction.

After completing all the religious ceremonies and other formalities following his wife's death, Paramaguru went back to his army life.

Sambandam, who was already a heart patient, couldn't take the strain of managing his coffee estate anymore and one day, walking up and down in the estate, he suffered a massive heart attack and died instantly, amidst his favorite coffee plant bushes. Paramaguru rushed back home. He realized that he was now responsible for his old mother, his young daughter, and the plantation. He finally resigned from the army and moved back to Yercaud for good.

Dolly was nine at that time.

Since his mother was incapable of taking care of her young granddaughter, Paramaguru decided to admit Dolly in the Montford convent boarding school and made arrangements for her to come home on weekends.

Surprisingly he liked his life in Yercaud more than he had expected to. He began learning a lot about the newer varieties of coffee and how to grow them. He read about the subject, discussed it with friends, and enjoyed experimenting and implementing his learning.

He learnt about Arabica, Robusta, Liberica and other varieties of coffee, how to grow them and their export, from neighboring estate owners. Soon, they became his friends. After working hard the whole day, he felt good spending the evenings with his friends. They preferred coming over to Paramaguru's place because they were sure that his old and unwell mother wouldn't come out of her room and of course the delicious snacks that he served. Scotch flowed like water… there were cooks to serve whatever they asked for… interesting conversation… what else could one ask for.

The conversation would be normal till a few pegs were downed. After that one of them would lose patience, cut the conversation saying, "Major, you left that story about that model girl incomplete…"

That is all the sloshed Major needed…

Aha! Who can resist my mind blowing experiences! I have these guys begging for more…

Paramaguru would lose control and talk openly about things he should not be talking about.

Bhaskaran Nair is a forty year old bachelor. He had a lot of family responsibilities and had to take care of his siblings. He had worked very hard and had never had the opportunity to experience the other side of things in life and was unaware of the outside world.

Seth is a fifty year old family man. He owns a big house and a superstore in Salem but came to Paramaguru's house regularly, not wanting to miss the titillating stories he narrated.

Apart from these two, there were Ravi and Daniel and a few others who listened to Paramaguru's stories with mouths wide open. They couldn't believe that such things were even possible.

It was a Friday. It was an unexpected holiday and the gang had assembled earlier than usual.

The drinking session that began at lunch got extended and none of them had eaten well. When they opened the

Scotch that evening, everyone was totally inebriated. For some reason Paramaguru was very happy that day.

Daniel, who was completely drunk said, "You must narrate some new story Major... not your usual stuff."

Paramaguru was more than happy.

"Alright, I will tell you something unusual... OK?" He lowered his voice to a whisper and said, "Remember, I had gone to that planters conference last week? That is where this happened. My friend is a senior teacher in a reputed school there.

He told me, "There is a fresh girl... a twelfth grade student... she comes from a poor family... aspires to be a doctor... I forced her to agree to my conditions and threatened her saying that I would cut her grades... stop her scholarship, and shatter her dreams.... She had no choice and agreed meekly... I will bring her to you... enjoy".

"I went to the place he mentioned. Believe me; I can never forget that experience ever in my life... an affair to remember... A young teenager... must be hardly sixteen... she was sweating with fear... but she had come out of compulsion... first time... Oh! It was the most incredible experience!"

When Paramaguru was describing his experience vividly with passion, Bhaskaran, who sat still, listening to every word intently, suddenly put his glass down, and stood up.

"What is the matter?"

"Nothing... I had committed to meet someone at seven this evening. I just forgot. I have to leave Major."

Bhaskaran rushed not even waiting for Paramaguru's response. The others too got up saying, "We also have to leave. It is getting late."

The next day, Saturday, was when Lakshmi came home for the weekends.

Paramaguru woke up early, got ready, and came to the living room at eight O'clock to welcome his daughter.

Being an army man, Paramaguru was a stickler for time and wanted everything to happen with clockwork precision. He had instructed the driver that he should leave with the car at seven thirty and be back with Dolly at eight O'clock sharp.

He was pacing in the garden waiting to see his daughter after a week's gap.

Eight O'clock.

The car returned but Dolly was not in it.

"She was not in school. The watchman said she had left early, in another car in the morning."

What? Guru thought, raising his eyebrows.

In some other car…? Whose car could it be? Where could she have gone? Maybe to some friend's house…

Whatever the reason may be, she shouldn't have gone somewhere without informing him. He was getting angry at Dolly. She was just thirteen but still shouldn't she be more responsible?

He called on his daughter's mobile. It was switched off.

He went in and sat at the dining table for his breakfast. He was sad because this was the first time in the four years that he was without his daughter on a Saturday.

"Dolly will come only for lunch. Get me breakfast." He said to the servant.

Eleven O'clock.

He couldn't concentrate on his book... where could she have gone? All her close friends lived in Salem which was quite a distance from Yercaud.

Shall I try calling them? As he pulled out his phoned from his pocket impatiently, he heard the sound of a car stopping at the gate briefly and leaving

"Da... dd... yyyyyy"

Paramaguru ran to the main door.

His daughter, his darling Dolly came running from the gate. Her hair was disheveled, her face swollen, streaked with tears!

"Oh My God! What happened?"

"Daddy," His daughter screamed as she came running through the portico, climbed the steps and fell into his arms.

"Da... dd..yy.."

For a moment Paramaguru was stunned and didn't know what to say.

"What happened..? Tell me darling." Paramaguru asked anxiously.

"That... That Bhaskar uncle... uncle... he came to school... said that you have asked him to pick me up... I went with him... he stopped the car in an isolated place... and... and... Oh Daddy! How can I say it... he... he..."

The ground slipped from under Paramaguru's feet.

His universe came crashing down on him...

His daughter wailed uncontrollably burying her face in his chest...

"Daddy... when he dropped me at our gate, he shouted...

"All because of your father… I am doing this only because of your father… go and tell him… he is responsible…"

"Why did he behave like this Daddy? Why was he saying that?"

Dolly wept, hitting her head against her father's chest.

God's mills had ground slowly but surely…

Gods waited and punished Paramaguru that Saturday morning.

2021

Misplaced Anger

Soon after breakfast, Saravanan picked up the bike keys and the lunch bag that Mohana kept on the table and got ready to leave.

"I am leaving."

Mohana followed him till the gate without saying a word.

Saravanan wore his gloves and helmet, started his bike and raised his hand gesturing 'bye'. After he left, Mohana sat on the steps, leaning on the wall.

She didn't feel like entering the house or eating. She was in no mood to do anything.

She seemed to be getting more and more annoyed with every passing second.

She too had been a working woman till seven months ago; the two of them used to leave for work together…

She sat thinking wistfully.

She would wake up early in the morning, cook breakfast, and lunch and pack their lunch boxes. They would have breakfast together, and leave for work on the bike. Saravanan would drop her to the office on the way. She worked as a receptionist in a private company in Pallavaram while he worked as a manager in a transport company in Royapettah.

It had been three years since they had got married. They had no children and were in no hurry to have them. They were happy and content indeed.

However, soon after they were married, when they moved to Srinagar colony, an upcoming middle class locality in the interiors, about two kms from Tambaram, she was indeed a little scared.

Though it was called a colony; there was only one more house other than theirs.

"I had money and so I built this house. The people who bought the land with me have taken bank loans. They will start constructing their houses as soon as their loans are sanctioned. Believe me; this colony will be full in a year's time." Saravanan said, trying to comfort her.

What he said was right... Though the colony wasn't full, seven or eight houses had come up within a year. Most importantly, her neighboring house got ready and Sharada came to live there with her large family. In fact Mohana didn't find too much time to interact with them, but she was relieved and happy to have them as noisy neighbors.

Saravanan and Mohana would leave for work in the morning and return home together in the evening. They would stop at the Tambaram market on the way and buy vegetables, fruits, grocery, idli batter and other daily needs.

Sundays were more relaxed. They would wake up at leisure. Mohana would have her weekly oil bath. They would have their favorite weekend lunch of onion sambar and potato fry, have a short nap, and go for a movie in the evening at the cinema theater in Tambaram. This was their regular weekend routine and Mohana was aware that Sharada was a little jealous of her.

But their happy and peaceful life was completely disrupted with the Corona pandemic hitting the world!

Even when the 'full lockdown' was announced in the third week of March, Saravanan and Mohana didn't think much about it. They took it as a 'month's leave' and enjoyed being at home together, cooking new dishes, playing carrom board, watching TV while enjoying hot bhajis and pakodas as evening snacks.

However, all that was short-lived and lasted only for ten days…

Within the next ten days, all the shops, hotels, public places, offices, and transport services like autos, taxis, and buses were completely stopped. Only after the movement of people on the streets was also banned, did the seriousness of the situation hit them.

Mohana's office shut down completely and she lost her job. Saravanan was getting only half his salary. They realized that they had to tighten things and cut down on their expenses. They followed the lockdown restrictions and remained indoors.

Once a week, Saravanan would go to the Tambaram market wearing gloves and a face mask to get whatever vegetables and groceries. Mohana would soak all the vegetables in water containing salt and turmeric for some time, wash them well and then store them. In the meanwhile Saravanan would soak his clothes in disinfectant liquid, wash them, and have a bath.

Within two months they were miffed watching non-stop news about how Corona patients were being isolated and the way the dead were being tied in sacks and buried, with the family members not even getting a last glimpse of their loved ones.

Every time there was news about some members of a house showing Corona symptoms, the municipality officials would seal off the entire street with tin partitions. Things were so bad that Mohana couldn't even say hello to Sharada for a few weeks!

Not a soul stepped out of their homes.

Thankfully, the 'lockdown' was eased about three months later and Saravanan started going to work. On the first of the month, they got a full month's salary after a long time!

How long is this situation going to continue?

Till when will they have to suffocate indoors and be imprisoned in their own homes?

A week ago, she thought it would be a good change for her to visit her parents or in-laws for some time.

That evening she asked Saravanan during dinner,

"Shall we go to Madurai, to your parents' place or visit my parents in Tirunelveli for Diwali? We have been stuck at home for the past six months and I feel I will go mad."

Saravanan stopped eating and looked at her intently,

"The bus and train services have just resumed and I don't think anyone has made plans for travel as yet. Even yesterday, some people who had come to our office to book a truck said that there is a possibility of a second wave and we should be careful. Why do you want to invite trouble? Let's not go now. We will plan something during the Pongal festival, in January…"

Mohana heaved a long sigh

She felt very irritated and disappointed at Saravanan refusal. The more she thought about the situation, the irritation in her soon turned into anger.

She bit her lips to control her anger and as she got up to go to the kitchen she noticed a row of small black ants crawling in a disciplined line along a crack on the floor. They went straight and disappeared into a hole in a corner close to the main door.

An ant hill! Oh! This is their hideout!

These ants were harmless and didn't sting but they attacked anything sweet! God knows how they are able to enter the sugar container in the kitchen. They find the container even if it is moved to another place.

Mohana was reminded of how she had to throw away a good amount of sugar in the sink that morning because it was full of ants.

"These pests- horribile ants!"

Her anger and annoyance peaked and she cursed them to her heart's content.

These ants were incorrigible. Nothing seemed to work against them. She had tried using varieties of pesticide sprays repeatedly, but Lo! They kept coming back. She was bent upon chasing the ants away.

How?

Suddenly she remembered reading somewhere that ants are able to follow each other owing to their sense of smell.

Aha! Now I know what to do!

Leaning forward, Mohana deliberately drew an invisible line across the path of the ants.

The ants were taken by surprise at their path being disturbed and they ran helter-skelter. She drew another line at a distance and the ants just scattered all over the place, forgetting their discipline, completely losing their path.

When Mohana went closer to the corner, she saw a group of ants pulling a small, dead moth towards the ant hill.

The anger bubbling inside made her bend down and knock the moth with her finger. It went and fell two feet away. The ants near the ant-hill were utterly confused and went round and round, not knowing what to do.

Mohana derived vicarious pleasure watching the ants in distress.

She felt a deep sense of satisfaction for having sought her revenge. She got up, shut the door, and went inside.

Saravanan's plate and glass lay on the table. Mohana dumped them hard, carelessly with a clang into the sink and left the kitchen in a huff.

She took two idlis disinterestedly on a plate from the container on the dining table and came to the living room. She switched on the TV but every single channel was showing only Corona related news....

'The second wave had begun in Europe...'

'Germany, France, and a few other countries impose lock down again...'

Chee!

She was disgusted.

Isn't there any other news except Corona?

As she flipped channels, she heard a Psychiatrist speaking on one of the channels,

"Misplaced Anger"

The word caught her attention and she continued watching.

"Misplaced anger" is very common amongst us- if our boss or senior berates us in office, we are not able to express our anger at him or her. We come home and vent our anger on our spouses. If a husband shouts or abuses his wife, the helpless wife ends up beating up her children for no reason. Such acts that we do unintentionally are because of misplaced anger. When we are incapable of standing up to, or expressing our annoyance and anger at people who are more powerful or senior to us; we take out our frustration and anger at people who can't fight us or are weaker than us. This is misplaced anger. Come to think of it, all of us have at some time or the other behaved like this…"

Mohana couldn't bear to listen to the Psychiatrist any longer. She put her plate on the table and straightened up with a start.

Misplaced anger

Did I just take out my frustration and anger against Saravanan and Corona on those helpless, mute ants?

She sat numbed for a few moments.

She took a piece of idli from her plate, covered it with sugar, opened the door, and walked towards the anthill. She went close to the place where the ants were crawling in a disciplined line once again. She squatted down, broke the idli into small bits and scattered it around the hole. She picked up the dead moth lying two feet away and placed it near the ant hill remorsefully and whispered 'sorry' repeatedly.

With the irritation and anger that was boiling inside subsiding, Mohana felt like crying.

2021

Migrants

The heat radiating through the tin roof was unbearable. Muthaiyyan sat up and looked at the fuzzy silhouettes of his wife Selvi, and Jyothi lying next to him. Both of them had lost a lot of weight due to lack of nutrition and care. Selvi is pregnant after a gap of four years. She is in her fifth month now. Muthaiyyan felt like crying and a lump formed in his throat thinking about his helplessness and inability to provide two square meals to his pregnant wife and three year old daughter.

He got up, noiselessly opened the tin door, came out and sat on the plastic chair kept near the door.

There was a line of tin-roofed shacks like a goods train. There were a few tall under- construction buildings a little distance away. The Medical College, Engineering College, Arts College with their students' hostels, guest houses, auditorium and other buildings looked like ghostly shadows under the dim light of the street lamps.

The private University campus being built on a hundred acre plot was proposed to open in July with a grand inauguration ceremony.

But how…?

The cursed Corona pandemic had brought all work to a standstill on the 25th of March.

Muthaiyyan felt restless and walked between the rows of shacks. Some people were sleeping on rope cots outside, not being able to bear the heat indoors. The builders had given each worker a 10 by 10 feet, single-roomed, tin shack separated by a short distance. There were few bathrooms and toilets a short distance away.

There were almost three hundred laborers living there of which, only thirty were from Tamilnadu, from cities like Salem and Trichy and about ten from Kerala. The rest were all from Bihar, Orissa and West Bengal. There were very few workers who had come with families like Muthaiyyan had.

While walking in the semi-darkness, Muthaiyyan noticed that a lot of the shacks were vacant.

How much has changed in the last one month!

The company disbursed the salary on 1st April and announced, "We can't give you salaries anymore. We have no idea when the construction will resume. You may decide what you want to do." Even after that firm announcement, nobody thought things would get worse so fast.

The bus and other transport services stopped and it became difficult to even go to the town fifteen kms away and buy groceries and vegetables. Walking 15 kms up and down in the April heat was killing!

When the bus services were operational, a milk vendor would come and deliver milk at their doorstep. Now, they had to buy milk powder for their children and have black coffee themselves. Soon all supplies they had, got exhausted and they had to survive on just one meal a day. By 15th April, the situation in the colony became really grim.

The company turned a blind eye and a deaf ear to their problems. The two security guards of the godowns had no information and they were in deep trouble themselves.

In the meantime the laborers were getting all kinds of news on their mobile phones.

On one side was the encouraging news of 'A lone migrant labourer from Hyderabad walking 1000 kms and reaching Sivagangai in ten days and on the other, was the depressing news of 'sixteen people who were walking along the railway lines, sleeping on the tracks due to exhaustion and dying when a goods train ran over them' or that of 'eight people dying when a speeding truck crushed them while they were walking on the highway.'

By 20th April, hunger and starvation struck the colony and the laborers from the North decided to leave come what may. Some of them who had bicycles, loaded their stuff and rode towards home, while others decided to walk home thinking it was better to die at home than die there of starvation.

Only a few Tamil family men like him and some elderly people stayed back.

Whatever money they had saved over the last two years was there in the bank accounts they had opened in the bank in the town. But, they would have to walk 30 kms up and down to get the money. Even then there was no guarantee that the banks and the grocery shops would be open.

What was the point in having money if they couldn't buy anything? How long was this misery going to last? Days? Months? How will they go home if they spent all their money here itself?

Muthaiyyan got vexed thinking about all this; he came back and sat on the chair feeling dejected and homesick.

Muthaiyyan belonged to a small village called Pallipalayam, near Cuddalore, just off the highway, a half an hour walk from the main road. The village had only two streets, one with potters and the other where the Reddys and Naickars lived. At the end of the streets was the Pavadairayan temple.

His father passed away when Muthaiyyan was just sixteen. He decided to quit studies and learn pottery. Muthaiyyan was hard working and sat on the potter's wheel for hours on end making close to forty clay pots and containers per day.

His mother would collect the clay from Vadhikaal and Thethaangarai and soak it overnight.Muthaiyyan would wake up at the crack of dawn and stamp the wet clay with his feet and knead it. He would have some leftover rice around nine O'clock and sit on the wheel. He planned his day's activities meticulously and would get up only after making thirty or forty pots.

Even his grandfather commented frequently to Muthaiyyan's mother, "The way your son is going, looks like he will be able to build his own tile-roofed house very soon."

But all his dreams came crashing down and were washed away by the cyclone 'Gaja' in 2011.

Torrential rains coupled with heavy winds... the sea swelled and the high waves came crashing into his house. His mother, sleeping in the kitchen, got stuck between the debris and died. Muthaiyyan who was sleeping on the other side survived miraculously. The village, its people, cattle, the trees... everything that had existed till the previous night had vanished in the morning...

His maternal uncle and aunt, who had come to visit him, consoled the shaken Muthaiyyan. They stayed back till the last rites for his mother were completed and took him along with them to Senthamangalam. It was a village on the banks of the Kaveri near Thiruverumbur. His uncle had a banana plantation on a two acre plot. Muthaiyyan took up the responsibility of the plantation, interacted with people who had studied agriculture and learnt ways of improving the yield. The earnings that were twenty five thousand rupees a year soon grew to forty five thousand rupees. He was twenty five years old when he married his uncle's daughter Selvi three years later. Selvi conceived and soon gave birth to their daughter Jyothi.

His friends suggested that he should plant the red variety of bananas and they could double the earnings by exporting them. Muthaiyyan went to Kerala, bought the specific saplings, took the neighboring plot on lease and planted red banana plants on the three acre plot. He took loans to buy fertilizers, pesticides and the plants grew healthy and tall and were ready to fruit within ten months.

While they waited in anticipation, cyclone 'Vardah' hit the Tamilnadu coast on the 9th and 10th December, 2016 and all the banana trees collapsed and perished.

Before he could blink, all his hard work had been blown away in a flash. Not giving time to recover from the calamity that hit him, the money lender came knocking at his door demanding his money back. Even after mortgaging all the jewelry, Muthaiyyan was unable to clear all his debts.

What could he do? How was he going to repay the remaining debt? He needed money to make his land arable and he was at his wits end. That was when Murugesan from the next street came with an agent.

"Even my land is devastated and I too am struggling to make ends meet. This is a friend of my brother-in-law in

Karur. They are looking for construction labor to work in Andhra Pradesh. They will pay ten thousand rupees and provide free accommodation and food. It will be a two year contract and they will pay a twenty five thousand rupees advance. I have decided to repay my loans with that amount and go."

Murugesan was a bachelor and could go without any hassles. But, Muthaiyyan had a wife and child to think about. He thought a lot and felt that it was possible. He decided to leave Selvi and Jyothi at his uncle's place and go alone. But the agent argued, "Why? Let them also come! They pay 8000 rupees for female laborers. Why do you want to let go of that? There is a child care center in the colony itself where they will take care of all the small children. If you leave your children there in the morning, they will feed them, give them milk and take care of them till you return from work."

Ten and eight… eighteen thousand, plus the child will be taken care of. It was a matter of only two years! That will pass in a flash… And it's not as if we are going abroad. It is only in Andhra, which is close by…

From the twenty five thousand rupees advance, Muthaiyyan paid the remaining debt of twenty thousand rupees and bought two sets of new clothes for himself, Selvi and Jyothi, and gave his uncle two thousand rupees saying, "Give the land on lease Uncle. I will send you money every month."

Muthaiyyan, Selvi and Jyothi left for Chennai by bus with Murugesan and Ekambaram's family. The agent bought them food and helped them board the train to Hyderabad along with the other laborers who had come from Karur and Salem.

They got down at Hyderabad the next morning. They had the breakfast that was given to them and traveled to the construction site by bus. The ride took two hours. They were building a 100 acre private university campus. There were many other laborers from the North. They could see a compound wall around with only the foundations of a few buildings erected. Otherwise it was barren land.

The moment they reached, they were asked to take a bath and were given lunch packets. They were then taken to the nearby town fifteen kilometers away and asked to open bank accounts in the local bank. With the advance of two thousand rupees, they bought groceries, vegetables, kitchen utensils, pots and pans.

The contractors realized that if workers from the same state, speaking the same language were kept together, they would waste a lot of time chatting and start criticizing the company. The laborers were sent to separate shacks and made to work on different buildings to ensure that they couldn't talk to anyone freely or make friends.

On the very third day they realized that the promise of free food and housing was an eye wash. The tin shacks were shown as houses and the contractor announced rudely, "We will give you 5 kgs of rice every month. You cook your meals yourselves."

Work started on the fourth day. They had to report for work at 8 am and were allowed to go home for lunch at 1 PM. They would resume at 3 PM and work till 7 in the evening. The work was back breaking and tough. Jyothi's daycare was also in a tin shack and a middle aged Telugu woman was there to take care of the children. However they gave the children a glass of milk, some rice, and an egg every day, which was reasonable.

Muthaiyyan was not used to mixing cement, mortar and gravel and within a week his hands and feet were completely bruised and full of sores. The flimsy rubber slippers hardly lasted for ten days. The workers tore strips of the empty cement sacks and tied them on their feet for protection. By the time they returned from work utterly exhausted, bathed, cooked and ate, it would be 10 o'clock at night.

The next shock that awaited them was the first month's salary. The contractors showed accounts for the advance, house rent, child care and other expenses and gave Muthaiyyan only twelve thousand rupees in place of the promised eighteen thousand rupees. He was shocked beyond imagination!

"We are ruined, Muthu. They promised a lot and this is what they have done! We are stuck… We have signed on the two year contract as well. We can do nothing but work quietly for two years…" lamented Murugesan. Muthaiyyan didn't know what to say.

He sent two thousand rupees to uncle and kept five thousand for his daily expenses. He deposited the remaining five thousand rupees in the bank.

Muthaiyyan's plans of saving one lakh twenty thousand rupees in two years at five thousand rupees a month too didn't materialize owing to the twenty five thousand rupees he had to send for uncle's intestinal surgery and almost ten thousand spent for Jyothi's hospitalization when she had Typhoid. Unexpected expenses pounced on him from all directions and he was left with only forty thousand rupees in his bank account.

He decided that he would go back home with whatever was left once his contract expires in June, but that too seemed like a pipedream with the Corona pandemic. Their lives had been devastated in the last two months.

"Mama, why are you sitting outside so early?" Selvi came out rubbing her sleepy eyes and sat next to him.

"Have you thought about what Murugesan Anna had suggested?"

"Mm… yes… We should leave…"

Murugesan had come to meet them four days ago. His eyes were blazing red and his face was sullen.

"Anna, where have you disappeared? Haven't seen you for four days! You are keeping well, aren't you?" Muthaiyyan asked with concern.

"I have a bad cold… my Bengali neighbor's son has had a fever for the past one week. I took him to the town on my bicycle and admitted him to the hospital there. Since there was no one to buy him milk, food and medicines, I stayed back with him. He was feeling a little better; hence I left my cycle with him and walked back today. I am feeling dead tired and there is nothing at home. Selvi, can I have some hot water?"

Selvi made some black tea and gave him a tablet for fever.

Murugesan came back again the previous day and said, "When I was in the town, I met the lorry driver Reddy who transports cement for us. He said that our owner is a kind hearted man and feels very bad for all of us stuck here. If all of us agree, he can take us by truck and help us reach Chennai via Ongole and Nellore. The other Tamil and Malayali laborers are ready to go. It will cost 4000 Rs. per person and there will be no charge for children. Let us take this as a path shown by our Lord Pavadairayan and leave. Shall I tell them that you too are ready?"

The plan was to leave on the coming Tuesday and reach Chennai by eight O'clock on Wednesday morning.

The menfolk shook off their exhaustion, walked together to the town and withdrew the required amount of money from their bank accounts. Muthaiyyan withdrew 12000 Rs. He enquired if the remaining amount in his account could be transferred to the bank in his village. He bought a kg of rice, half a liter of milk, biscuit packets and bananas. After having bought all the important stuff, he gave Reddy 8000 Rs for himself and Selvi.

By the time they came back to the camp, Murugesan could hardly walk another step. His fever had shot up and he coughed incessantly. He somehow struggled his way to the camp. Selvi gave him a cup of hot tea and medicine for his fever. The next morning Muthaiyyan went to Murugesan's shack to give him some hot porridge and said to Selvi worriedly when he came back, "Anna's face is very dull… I hope we reach home safely."

They bathed, took their food stuff, water bottles, packed their good clothes in their trunk and got ready to leave. They boarded the truck with their belongings. There were twenty six people including seven women and children. The women were made to sit towards one side and the men stood towards the front of the truck. Muthaiyyan helped Murugesan into the truck and made him lie down on one side.

Since they would have to pay a lot of toll tax if they took the highway and there would be a lot of police checking as well, the truck driver decided to drive through narrow, bumpy inner village roads.

"We have to travel 640 kms. It will take us 15 hours to reach Chennai via Nallakonda, Athangi, Ongole and

Nellore. All of you just lie down wherever you can. It is getting dark." Veluswamy announced loudly and firmly.

Murugesan's persistent cough sounded jarring in the silence of the night and everyone was getting annoyed. Murugesan tried to stuff the end of his towel into his mouth to stop his coughing but it was no use. After traveling for four hours, Reddy stopped the truck in a small village, on the side of the road. All of them got down, urinated under the trees and behind the shrubs, ate a little, stretched themselves for some time and left.

"The truck will not stop anywhere from now onwards. Reddy says we have to reach Ongole in five hours."

They curled up within the space in the truck and tried to sleep. Murugesan couldn't even lie down. His body was raging with fever and his cough was worse. He started groaning.

"Shall I give you some water Anna?" Muthaiyyan asked. Murugesan just said with difficulty, "I am not able to breathe... I can't take it anymore..."

When Muthaiyyan switched on the flashlight on his cell phone and looked at Murugesan's face, his lips were dry, face twisted and he was panting for breath. Veluswamy and a few others too woke up and were shocked to see Murugesan's state.

They panicked and asked Reddy to stop the truck. Reddy came and seeing Murugesan he said worriedly, "We will reach Ongole in another half an hour. We can admit him in the government hospital there. He seemed to be alright a few hours ago! What happened? Is he having chest pains?"

They reached Ongole as planned, went to the government hospital and helped Murugesan down and made him sit on a bench. The nurse from the emergency ward came out sleepily, rubbing her eyes. She had one look at Murugesan and said in Telugu, "Looks like a Corona case. He is in such a serious condition… move away… don't touch him."

Corona?

All the men standing around jumped back as if they had stepped on a snake. They wondered, 'We have traveled together for so long! God knows how many of us have caught it!'

There was utter commotion and turmoil for the next half an hour. The duty doctor had a look at Murugesan and called someone on his cell phone.

"We can't admit him and give him a 'bed' till the senior doctor comes and checks him. We may have to call an ambulance and take him to another hospital."

"Sir, there are women and children in my truck and it is my responsibility to ensure they reach Chennai safely. You kindly take charge of this person Sir, please." Reddy said pleadingly and handed some money to the attendant. The man took the money nodding his head.

Muthaiyyan felt sad and guilty leaving Murugesan alone like an orphan.

"Anna, shall I stay back with you?"

"No, you have a pregnant wife and child with you… You leave. I have money… Don't worry, I will manage." Murugesan said breathlessly.

Reddy generously sprayed the place Murugesan slept with sanitizer and by the time they left, the sun had come up and it was becoming hotter by the minute.

Selvi said sniffling, "Mama, what is this? We are going away, leaving Murugesan Anna all alone!"

Nellore was 140 kms from Ongole and they could reach there in two hours. When they were 10 kms away from Nellore, suddenly the truck shook violently and stopped with a big thud. The axle had broken.

"Major repair… We have to get another truck and tow this one away. I spoke to the owner. He asked me to give you back 1000 Rs each. If you all walk fast, you can reach Nellore in one hour." The sorrow and disappointment of not being able to keep his promise of seeing them home safely was evident in Reddy's voice.

All the passengers got down with their luggage, took the money and got ready to walk. Jyothi's slippers snapped as she jumped off the truck while Selvi felt a shooting pain in her lower back.

It was noon and the sun was right blazing overhead.

"There is no point waiting… Come on, all of you get going…" Veluswamy shouted.

Selvi said softly, "My back is hurting badly Mama."

"I am hungry." Said Jyothi

When Kadiresan's children also said they were hungry, they decided to stay back while the others started walking. Kadiresan and Muthaiyyan's family sat under a tree and opened their food packets. The fifty year old Manickam, who was struggling to walk because of painful corn in his feet, too stayed back. They had a few fists full of rice each, and drank all the remaining water they had. Manickam tore the towel he was carrying into two and tied it around the soles of his feet.

"It is getting late. Let us leave." Said Kadiresan standing up.

"You go ahead… we will come in some time…" said Muthaiyyan, taking out a towel from the trunk. He tore it in two halves the way Manickam did and tied it tightly around Jyothi's feet. They could see Kadiresan's family and Manickam walking far ahead.

"Get up Selvi… If they get very far, we will not have anyone to keep us company…"

Selvi got up with a moan and walked slowly holding her husband's shoulder for support. Her lower back was throbbing with pain. She bit her lower lip hard as she labored on. The food bag she was carrying felt heavy and she was breathless within ten steps.

"Appa, my feet are hurting…" wept Jyothi.

Muthaiyyan kept the trunk down and lifted Jyothi up on his shoulders. He began walking carrying the trunk in his left hand. He kept looking back and forth in the hope of getting a lift in some car or truck. But the road was empty except for an occasional car that whizzed past ignoring his extended hand.

"Appa, I want water. I am thirsty" Jyothi said repeatedly.

"Hold on for some time. Just swallow your saliva."

The bright sun rays hit his eyes and he could hardly keep his eyes open.

Kadiresan, his family and Manickam looked like small dots in the distance and soon disappeared from his sight.

Every step that Selvi took felt like she was walking on a bed of nails. She breathed deeply and when she took the next step a sharp, stabbing pain shot up in her lower abdomen.

"Ma…. ma…" It was an agonizing call.

The food bag slipped from her hands and she flopped on the ground with a thud groaning …'aaah… Aiyo… Ma… maa'.

Muthaiyyan who was walking four steps ahead put Jyothi down hurriedly, threw the trunk aside and ran back to his wife Selvi who was sitting crouched on the road… his eyes fell on a red puddle spreading beneath her folded legs.

2020

Reflections

He just couldn't sleep. He tossed and turned in his bed, but sleep eluded him. He got vexed and sat up

It was only three O'clock; he had to leave at seven thirty and there was a lot of time.

He walked out to the balcony and watched the full moon shining brightly like a silver plate in the sky. He sat on the swing and pushed it with his legs. He could see the white, star-shaped jasmine blooms hanging from the vines clearly in the moonlight. The sweet fragrance of the Parijatham blooms blended with the jasmine flowers and created an intoxicating fusion. Plucking the unopened jasmine buds, shaking the Parijatham tree and picking up the flowers and stringing them into garlands was one of Akila's favorite pastimes.

When he had returned from the Minister's public meeting, it was the fragrance of the Magnolia garland hanging on Akila's photo in the living room that welcomed him. He realized that Akila's parents must have brought the blooms from their garden in Trichy and made the garland. This was a regular feature of their visits to Chennai.

Raghavan and Shanti, who sat chatting with his mother in the living room, stood up as soon as they saw him.

"Please sit… don't bother to get up… I will just freshen up and be back in a minute,"

He went to his room, washed his face, changed his clothes and came to the living room.

"Did you have coffee and snacks?" He enquired as he sat down on the opposite couch.

"Yes, we did… How are you Sathya?"

"Fine. Thank you."

"Amma was saying that you have a lot of work these days."

Sathya just smiled,

"We both came together because we had to discuss something important with you."

"Tell me, Mama."

"People from the college Akila worked in had come to meet us. They requested us to help them build a state of the art science lab. We have decided to construct a separate building with a lab on the ground floor and a library on the first floor."

"That is wonderful, Mama."

"It is Akila's birthday on the 25th. We are planning to hand over the cheque for the building to them on her birthday. It would be nice if you could be present on the occasion."

Raghavan noticed Sathya's hesitation and continued, "There won't be a big crowd Sathya. Four persons from the trust will come and collect the cheque from us. They plan to have a grand inauguration ceremony once the building is ready."

Amma, who was listening quietly till then added, "It is a good cause Sathya. You should be present."

"There is one more thing Sathya," Raghavan said as Sathya looked at him quizzically.

"Akila, our only child was born eighteen years after our marriage. I am now seventy years old. Last month my friend Shankar, the owner of Shankar Structurals, died of a heart attack all of a sudden. He was healthy and had no health issues."

Sathya looked up at Raghavan wondering what he was getting at.

Raghavan came to the point saying, "We both want to register our shares and our wealth in your name. I will take care of the factory, the company and other ventures till I am alive. After that you can take over. We have a lot of experienced professionals to manage everything. You will not have any problems. You may decide to manage all the companies or decide to…"

Sathya interrupted, "Mama, wait a second. What is all the hurry for?"

"I have been thinking about this for a long time. It is not a sudden decision and I should have done this when Akila was alive.Somehow, I just didn't do it then. I was under the illusion that all of us are immortal." Raghavan's voice trembled.

"If you come by the morning flight on the 25th, we can call the college authorities at five O'clock in the evening. The next day, Wednesday, is an auspicious day and we can have the registration. I have already spoken to the lawyer and the advocate. You can complete all the formalities within two days."

Having said what he had to, Raghavan and his wife left after having dinner with Sathya.

Sathya knew this was coming… but how could one argue with someone who had lost his only daughter?

Sathya packed his suitcase, got ready and came down. He saw his mother waiting for him in the living room. She handed him the coffee brought by the cook Dhanam and asked, "Are you not going by flight? I see that the driver Thirumalai has come!"

"No… I will leave now… will be back the day after tomorrow."

He asked Thirumalai, who was loading the suitcase into the car, "Have you filled up petrol, and did you check the tyres?" Thirumalai nodded and Sathya held his hand out for the car keys.

"Thirumalai, you need not come. I will drive on my own."

"It is a long drive. Why are you asking him not to come?"

He smiled listening to his mother's worried voice.

"Don't worry Amma; it's been a long time since I went on a long drive. I will be careful."

Amma nodded, understanding that he desired to be alone.

He got into the car, shut off the AC and rolled down the windows.

He drove unhurriedly. Since it was reasonably early in the morning; there was hardly any traffic. The cool October breeze felt soothing on his face. The new airport shone bright with all the lighting.

He remembered that Akila would drop him and pick him from the airport on all his national and international trips. She would chuckle aloud whenever he asked, "Why do you bother at such odd hours?"

She used to get beautiful dimples every time she smiled and Sathya would deliberately make her smile just to see them.

As he crossed the "Sivananada Gurukulam' at Kattangulatthur, he remembered that all the children and the elders there would be wearing new clothes that day.

"When we wear new clothes on our birthday, wouldn't these children too feel like wearing new clothes as well, Sathya? When Appa asked me what gift I wanted for my 18th birthday, I named four ashrams and asked Appa to buy new clothes for all the children. Sivanada Gurukulanm was one of them. Sathya, every year when I see the happiness on the children's' faces, my joy knows no bounds!"

Akila had big eyes and they would become wider whenever she spoke with enthusiasm and passion. He would be reminded of a doe seeing her beautiful eyes.

"Before the Chengalpet bypass road was ready, we had to go through the nearby town. Once we saw a huge crowd around a tamarind tree. When we stopped to see what the matter was, we saw a man hanging from the tree. It was really frightening. The man's wife stood there crying aloud with her baby in her arms. God knows what trouble they were in! Why did he have to commit suicide? We went to the police station and informed them about the incident…"

Akila talked a lot but she never gossiped. She was always genuinely concerned about people. She would introspect deeply and come up with new thoughts and ideas.

Akila was born and brought up in Trichy and completed her education there. Since she had traveled from Trichy to Chennai a zillion times over the years; she knew every milestone on NH 45 like the back of her hand and remembered every incident that happened on the way over the years.

Today is Tuesday the 25th. It was on a Tuesday that he had met Akila for the first time. It must have been a few months since he had been posted at Trichy as the District Collector. Akila, who was working as a lecturer in one of the local colleges, had come to his office to invite him as the chief guest for the College day.

"She is industrialist Raghavan's daughter Sir. She does a lot of social work." Sathya's assistant had told him after she left.

After that the two met on several other occasions in the following months-while adopting a village, building toilets in slums, providing braille computers for blind students and many other social projects.

A bright, elegant and simple appearance, pleasant personality, intelligent and sharp wit, and a helping nature… Akila was grounded and never exhibited her wealthy background. Sathya was impressed by her simplicity and admired the way she went around unassumingly on her scooter and treated everyone with a smile.

Sathya had realized that she too felt something special for him the day her parents visited his place all of a sudden. Raghavan was a man who spoke straight and didn't mince words. He came to the point, addressing Sathya's mother.

"You must be surprised to see us here out of the blue. To put it simply, I run the factory set up by my grandfather. Akila is my only child. There is not much to say about us. I have found out everything about you and your family before I decided to come here. It is remarkable to see that you have single handedly managed to bring up your son very well despite losing your husband very early in life. He is a brilliant student and has been a rank holder throughout. Though he became a collector at a very young age, he is known to be an upright and honest officer. It will be an honor if your son becomes our son in law. We are aware that my daughter also likes him a lot…"

They got married in a simple ceremony the very next month.

Sathya got transferred to Chennai with a promotion to a senior post in the Finance department. They moved into a beautiful independent house with a small, lovely garden in Thiruvanmayur and started their married life in style. Their life was brimming with happiness.

Two years filled with laughter and contentment passed like two minutes.

Sathya crossed the arrow showing 'Vedanthangal' towards the right and stopped. He took a U-turn and went back a short distance.

When they were traveling to Trichy by car for the first time after their marriage, Akila too had stopped and turned the car similarly back towards Vedanthangal.

"This is summer… not the right time for birds dear."

"It's alright. Let us go and see Sathya. I have traveled on this road so many times but never got a chance to go to Vedanthangal. Please Sathya… please…"

They went.

They walked up to the bank of the lake in the blazing sun and all they could see was a dried up lake bed with a few buffaloes wading in the shallow pools of water.

This was the right season. Sathya stopped the car under a tree and began walking towards the lake. Even before he reached the bank, he could hear the chirping of a variety of birds. He saw innumerable birds… cranes, pelicans and other migratory birds from all over the world. He stood watching the birds for ten minutes and came back to his car. He got in, switched on the AC, pushed back his seat and stretched himself. He didn't feel like going anywhere or meeting anybody…

They had gone to Nepal for their second wedding anniversary. After sightseeing, when they sat for lunch, he noticed that she was struggling to swallow her food and sipping water with every mouthful.

"Is your throat hurting?'

"No."

"Why are you struggling to swallow your food?"

"It has been like this for some time now."

"Since when…?

"A month or so…"

Sathya felt angry with himself. They never had their lunch together because of work, but did manage to have dinner together. Why hadn't he noticed her problem all these days? Most of the time, he would get calls from the Minister or the secretary and he had to talk to them on the phone while eating his meals. Is that why he had overlooked her problem?

They went for a checkup to Apollo hospital immediately after they returned from Nepal.

"This could be because of acidity or gastric ulcers. Let's do an endoscopy to check the severity of the problem." The doctor said,

They did the endoscopy as well as a CT scan. It was stomach cancer that had spread to the liver… had reached the fourth stage!

They tried everything possible - Surgery, chemotherapy, radiation… to no avail.

"This is an aggressive form of cancer. It spreads very fast without any symptoms… Really sorry." The doctor said despairingly.

Even after she lost her hair, and became weak because of all the intense treatment, her dimpled smile remained intact.

"I am fine Sathya, I won't leave you ever…"

But…

They had experienced the happiness and companionship of a lifetime and done all the social work they could in the last two years. Was it because she had to go so soon?

As he crossed the Madhuranthagam bypass, he could see the top of the towering gopuram of the Erikaatha Rama temple. That was the temple Sathya and Akila had visited last. They had gone to Trichy to seek their parents' blessings just before leaving for Nepal. They had returned to Chennai the same day.

"Have you been to the Erikaatha Rama temple Sathya?"

"No".

"Shall we go now?"

It must have been six O'clock in the evening. The sun was still bright and the temple lamps hadn't been lit. The temple looked dull and jaded. A lone lamp burnt dimly in the sanctum sanctorum.

"We don't have healthy earnings like before Amma. We are struggling to make ends meet. We are not able to afford oil for all the lamps…" The priest lamented.

Akila took out the few thousand rupees she had in her bag and said handing the money to the priest, "please buy new clothes for everyone and light all the lamps in the temple. Henceforth I will send you money every month."

Sathya could still recall the boundless happiness on the priest's face. His eyes had gleamed with delight!

It was 1 o'clock in the afternoon. Sathya realized that his in-laws would be waiting for him to have lunch with them. He sent them a message saying, 'I will be late. Am stuck with some work... Please don't wait for lunch.' He switched off the phone knowing that they may call back.

Ulundoorpettai...

Perambalur...

Vaalikandapuram...

So many places... so many incidents... so many conversations...

As he neared Trichy, he could see the Srirangam temple on the right and the Thiruvaanaikaaval temple on the left. He stopped his car, got down and walked to the bridge. He walked to the edge of the bridge and sat on the ledge.

"Sathya, my mother used to sing a beautiful lullaby describing this place... It talks about the beauty of the river Kaveri flowing around Srirangam like a garland around Lord Vishnu's neck...

You know Sathya, she would sing the song set in Nilambari ragam so sweetly that I could listen to it for hours. I am going to sing the same lullaby for our child too!

But... Akila's dreams could never be fulfilled...

His heart felt heavy and Sathya blinked to keep his tears away.

It was getting late. The college trustees would arrive at five.

As Sathya reached his in-laws' place, the guard had kept the gate open expecting him to arrive. He had to drive past a winding pathway along green lawns to reach the portico where Raghavan and Shanti stood waiting to welcome him.

He could see the surprise on their faces seeing that he had driven down on his own without a driver.

They went in and sat in the living room. The servant came carrying a tray with coffee and juice.

"Why didn't you come with the driver Sathya? It would have been far more comfortable if you had come by filght?" Shanti asked hesitatingly.

Sathya just smiled while picking up the coffee.

"This is the first time you have come here since Akila's passing. Having seen you both together till now; it breaks my heart to see you alone and …" Shanti started in a painful voice.

Sathya stood up before she could complete what she had to say.

"I will have a quick shower and get ready. The trustees will be here anytime."

He walked towards the staircase that led to his room on the first floor and as he was ascending the final step he realized that he had left his cell phone downstairs and he turned to walk down.

While climbing down, he could hear his mother in law's agony-filled voice clearly.

"Here we are grieving about our daughter and missing her every single moment... but look at him! The moment

I start saying anything about Akila, he just walks away…
This puzzles me! Of course, I do agree that he is young,
is very busy, and has a lot of work related stress and other
distractions… But… but… that doesn't mean one can forget
his loved one completely and react like this?"

Sathya didn't want to hear anything more.

As his mother in law began crying softly; he quickly
turned around and noiselessly walked back up the stairs.

2020

Transformation

The first thing that caught my attention when I opened the newspaper was the announcement.

Mother's day-A celebrity expressing his gratitude for all that his mother had done for him. I remembered that May10th was not only Mother's day but my mother's birthday as well. Amma never celebrated her birthday. The most she did was to visit the temple with us in the evening. Amma didn't celebrate our birthdays in a big way either. She would buy us new clothes, send chocolates for school, and that was it. Even all this stopped after Appa's passing away.

'I am leaving for work'... Appa had said while leaving for the bank on his scooter... He met with a serious road accident and died on the spot. They bought the tall, big man who had left home with a smile, tied up in a bundle!

I was in my second year B.Com, my younger brother Raghu was in twelfth grade while my sister Vasu was in the tenth standard. Appa worked in a bank and Amma worked as a lecturer in a college. Ours was a sweet, peaceful family with a nice house on a small plot in Nanganallur. We had two coconut trees, a drumsticks tree in the backyard; a Parijatham tree and other flowering shrubs in the front yard.

But, our peace and happiness was shattered by Appa's sudden, untimely death. I still remember, even after forty long years, every word Amma had spoken to us once the ceremonies were completed. She had called the three of us to her bedroom and said,

"It is now that the three of you have to be responsible. Appa was not interested in accumulating wealth and houses for you. He believed that educating you well was the biggest asset he could give you and I too believe the same. You all must not get despondent because Appa is not there. You study as much as you want and remember, I will take care of everything. You must study hard and come up so well that you become a shining example for everyone. You must reach dizzying heights and become successful professionals. Will the three of you do this for Appa and me?"

We did as she wished. In fact, all of us exceeded Amma's expectations!

Amma didn't talk much. If you ask four questions, she would gently give one answer. She would just give a small 'Monalisa' smile if anyone spoke something frivolous. It wasn't always easy to find out what was going on in her mind. However, she had spoken her mind openly that day and the three of us had fulfilled her wishes.

I completed my degree and then finished my C.A in three years with a gold medal. Raghu went to IIT Madras and IIM Ahmedabad on a scholarship from Aditya Birla Foundation and ensured that Amma didn't have to spend a paisa on his education. Vasu did her M.A economics and stood first in the State. She then went to London School of Economics on a scholarship…

I folded the newspaper and placed it on the swing. Amma's birthday kept crossing my mind as I shaved and showered. It would be so nice to meet Amma in person and spend some time with her! She would be so happy, wouldn't she? When I had spoken to her two days ago, her voice had sounded unusually dull.

When I asked her if she was alright, she said, "I have no problem. Kasturi takes care of me very well and the food is also mild, without much spice and oil…"

"Then why are you sounding so dull Amma?"

"I don't know why… but I have been feeling a bit lonely lately. Anyway… forget it… I will be alright."

Amma was always like this. She never made a big issue of her problems; she would brush them away saying, "Just forget it… let it be."

Initially, I felt extremely guilty moving away from Amma, and I would go and see her once a week. With time, the guilt subsided and gradually my visits became once in a fortnight and then once a month. Have the recent Corona lockdown and the curbs in travel become convenient excuses?

When I came out, Kamali walked to me with a list and some money. "Visu, Will you help me? I enquired over the phone; M.M store has opened and will be open only till 1 o'clock. He said that we have to go and buy the groceries ourselves because he doesn't have staff for home delivery. Can you go and get these things?"

Our driver, gardener, house maid and other servants have not been coming for work for the past one month. Thanks to our live-in maid Valli, we have no problems with our meals. Earlier, the shops would take the list by phone and home deliver the groceries, but now either Kamali or I have to go and get them personally.

I am not used to doing any household chores, and honestly never had to. Kamali said handing me the list and the money, "You have to maintain social distance. You may have to stand in line and it may take time. Why don't you have breakfast and go?"

"Just give me the coffee."

"It is Amma's birthday today." I said softly, taking the coffee mug from her. There was no response.

"Thought of going and meeting…" Kamali did not let me complete. "To Tambaram? It is not possible to go without an E-pass Visu. The police will stop the car and catch you. Why do you want to get into trouble? Amma is fine there. Just talk to her on the phone."

I did what I have been doing for the past thirty five years. I didn't say a word and left with the car keys.

As soon as I completed my C.A, I got an opportunity to join the reputed Ram and Co for my internship. Seeing my capability, Shankararaman made me permanent and I had risen to Junior partner in the third year itself. He got his only daughter Kamali married to me and I inherited Ram and Co, his house and other assets following his death.

Kamali always talked a lot and made decisions for other people without even waiting for their approval or permission. Well, that is how she was brought up. On the contrary, I am like my mother. I don't speak much and avoid arguments of any kind and that habit of mine continues till today.

Raghu fell in love with Amritha, a Punjabi girl while studying in IIM. And it was an affair serious enough to go till marriage. She is the daughter of Ahluwalia Singh, the owner of a well-known construction company

They had a lavish five-day wedding with several ceremonies like Sangeet and Mehendi held in different five star hotels in Delhi. Amma didn't oppose one bit. She attended the wedding ceremonies like a guest, blessed the newlyweds and returned to Chennai with me. Later, she went and stayed with them for ten days when their first daughter was born. After that she has never been to Delhi all these years. My guess is that the Delhi winter, the Hindi language, the food and culture doesn't suit her.

Vasu's is a different story altogether. She joined London School of Economics as a lecturer after completing her Masters there. "I am not interested in either living in India or getting married. I will come and visit Amma and you all whenever I feel like seeing you. You too can come here whenever you wish." All Amma had to say in response to Vasu's words was, "Is she a small child? She has decided what she wants. What matters is her happiness…"

"Why don't you come with me? Do you need to live alone like this?" I had asked Amma several times.

"No Visu, I am very comfortable in this house. I have a lot of friends here; there are temples and shops close by. It is a familiar place. We can always meet on festivals and special occasions." She never left the Nanganallur house.

But a few years ago, she fell down unexpectedly, broke her hip bone and had to undergo surgery. She was forced to come and stay with me. A separate room, a full-time nurse to take care of her… everything was comfortable and fine except for the fact that for some reason Kamali just didn't like Amma, although she never interfered in anything. For some unfathomable reason Kamali just couldn't be close to my mother. Was it because Kamali came from a very well to do family? Was it because Amma didn't know how to socialize like her mother? Was it because Amma didn't speak much? Whatever the reason, things became really ugly during that one year Amma stayed with us. Kamali wouldn't even peep into Amma's room for days. When Amma came into the dining room for her meals with the help of her walker; Kamali would get up and go saying, "I am not hungry, I will eat later."

Sometime last year, one day when I was busy with office work, Raghu and Vasu spoke to me over a conference call. They didn't mince words and came straight to the point. "Manni finds taking care of Amma a big burden. She might also be feeling sad that she is not able to go and stay with her daughter in Canada because of Amma. Vasu and I have spoken about this several times between ourselves. Expecting Amma to come and stay with us in London or Delhi is also out of the question. There is an assisted retirement home in Tambaram, Chennai. My friend's parents are also staying there.

They have 24/7 doctors, nurses and other medical facilities. They provide wholesome, healthy food suitable for senior citizens... we have found out all the details. It costs around 60,000 Rs a month... That is not a big amount and we will take care of it. We feel Amma will be more comfortable and peaceful there because she will have company of her age. We can come to Chennai next week and complete all the formalities. What do you say?"

What could I say? What were called 'old age homes' are being called 'retirement homes' these days! They are all the same except for some additional facilities.

Vasu and Raghu want me to be like those children who have settled abroad leaving their parents in such retirement homes, washing their hands off all responsibilities. Is this a western sensibility where one can live a guilt-free life leaving old parents in retirement homes?

It was clear as daylight to me that Kamali must have spoken to them and the three of them would have decided to do this.

I had reached the M.M store and saw people waiting in a long line maintaining social distance norms. Will it take an hour? I parked the car two houses away under a tree.

While I was stepping out of my car with my bag in hand, I saw a car stop in front of the next house. A man got out of the car, opened the gate, came back to the car, got in and parked it inside the gate.

Santhanam!

What is he doing here?

"Santhanam!"

He turned around, "Visu!" He said surprisedly.

"How come you are here?" he asked.

"I am the one who should be asking that. You had been to Australia to be with your son? When did you come back to Chennai? Whose house is this?"

Santhanam gave a friendly smile. "Come in. There is a lot to talk about."

I hesitated a little. "No, Kamali has given me a list of things to buy from M.M stores. They will close at one…"

"Give me the list." He said taking the list and money from my hand. He called the boy who was unloading the bags from his car,

"Raju, come here. Go to the M.M store and get all these things."

"Sir, I haven't changed the diaper for your father and haven't given him breakfast yet."

"I will take care of all that. You go."

We went into the house…

The last time I met Santhanam was when his wife died. Santhanam and I were neighbors in Nanganallur. We went to the same college and did C.A together. I joined Raman and Co while he joined the Reliance Company. He rose fast in the company and worked as a Vice President in Mumbai. We spoke to each other once in a while and met whenever possible. He lived a luxurious life with a flat in Marine Drive, two cars, drivers, and an army of servants.

His wife Vimala developed a severe kidney problem and died all of a sudden three years ago. I had gone to Mumbai when I got the sad news of her death. In the following months, I got busy with Amma's hip fracture and hadn't been in touch with him ever since.

"I have resigned from my job and I plan to live with my son in Australia." He had told me some time ago. I was meeting him for the first time after that.

His father was sitting on a wheelchair while his mother sat on the sofa in the living room. His mother looked at me blankly, not being able to recognize me. His father said, "Visu" in a garbled voice. His mouth drooled as he spoke.

What happened? Both of them were healthy and fine when I met them three years ago!

Santhanam could understand my shock. He came close to me and whispered, "Appa has severe Parkinson's disease and Amma has Alzheimer's. Both had very mild symptoms, but got worse very fast."

He went to his mother and hugged her warmly saying, "This is our Visu… Our neighbor, Eswar Mama's son." His mother asked again, "Which Visu?"

"I will tell you in detail once I change Appa's diaper and give him breakfast." Santhanam replied and turned towards his father. "Appa, Raju said your diaper needs to be changed. Come; let me change it for you." He lifted his father like a child. He turned towards me saying, "Give me two minutes" and walked towards the bedroom. Through the open door of the bedroom I could see him lay his father on the bed, remove his veshti and the diaper, wipe him clean, apply talcum powder, tie a new diaper, and dress him. He then brought his father back to the living room and rested him on the wheel chair.

He asked the nurse, "Why hasn't Appa had his breakfast?" "He said he will wait for you Sir."

He pushed the wheelchair towards the dining room saying "Appa, it is already late" while the nurse helped his mother to the dining table.

"Come, join us Visu. It's a long time since we have eaten together." I couldn't refuse and sat down.

"Saradamma, get the breakfast."

He tied a small towel like a baby's bib around his father's neck. The nurse fed his mother the idli while he fed his father small pieces of idli and said, "I lost interest in everything after Vimala died. I resigned from my job and went to Australia. I became restless within two months. I traveled around for some time there. I came back and went to Rishikesh to the Sivananda ashram; that too didn't work. Once I returned to Chennai, I realized that both Amma and Appa were in bad shape. I chided myself for wandering around without taking care of them. I felt extremely guilty for my behavior. I sold my Mumbai house, wound up everything, and moved here six months ago. I couldn't keep them very comfortable in the Nanganallur house so, I bought this house last month and moved here. There is Raju to take care of Appa, she is there for Amma, and Saradamma is there for cooking. I am no longer restless and feel happy and peaceful."

Once his father finished eating, Santhanam patiently wiped his face and fed him water. Santhanam went to his mother who sat vacantly. He took the spoon from the nurse.

"Amma, do you know who this is? He is the same guy who you used to scold saying, "This fellow is like a temple bull. The moment he gets a holiday, he is out roaming the streets. He is the same Visu Amma. Remember, you bought us identical shirts for Diwali once?"

Santhanam went on talking in an attempt to make his mother remember. He picked up the food particles that fell from her mouth and kept them on one side of the plate. He gave her sips of water in between and wiped her mouth with a napkin.

The more I watched Santhanam go about caring for his parents; it looked like a mother taking care of her children. I could feel a sudden uneasiness creep into me.

"Why aren't you eating Visu?"

"I had breakfast at home before I left." I said in a low voice.

"Ok, I have only been talking only about myself. Tell me, how is Amma? Nanganallur Balu Mama told me that you had taken her with you when she fell down and had a hip fracture… How are Kamali and the children? Have you changed your mobile number? I have not been able to contact you at all…"

Raju came back with two bags of the things Kamali had wanted me to buy. He handed me the bill and the change.

Sensing my increasing restlessness, I got up saying, "It is getting late Santhanam. I have some urgent work to do. Let me take your leave. My mobile number had got hacked and that is why I had to change it. Give me your number; I will give you a missed call. Now that you have moved here, we can meet and catch up frequently, Ok? Mama, see you soon, Mami, bye. See you Santhanam."

I saved his mobile number, loaded the grocery bags in the car and left in a hurry. For some reason, my eyes were welling up with tears, my throat was choked. My fingers shivered as I inserted the key to start the car.

I stopped the car on one corner of the street and called my friend Damodaran who is the Inspector General of police.

I came home.

"Was it too crowded?" Asked Kamali as I walked in… I stared at her for a few seconds.

"I am going to meet Amma after breakfast. Damu has told me he will send the E-pass home. I will have lunch with Amma and you don't wait for me…"

I could feel a confidence and resolve in my voice that I hadn't felt for many years.

2020

The Bodhi Tree

She shifted the heavy vegetable basket from her right hand to the left and went into the medical store. She just had to buy a tin of 'Cerelac' for her baby. Her infant daughter was asleep when she left home. Usually, it was Vasu who bought all the daily needs and he volunteered to do the same that day too, but she had stopped him.

"You leave it… I will go today and be back in half an hour. I feel like going out and getting some fresh air. The baby is sleeping. I have kept her milk ready in the bottle. Just warm it and feed her if she wakes up…"

The corner vegetable vendor close to her house was closed; she bought the vegetables from the store on the main road and came to the medical shop. There were two people at the counter and she turned her gaze around the street as she waited for her turn.

There was a lot of activity four buildings away across the road. Bright lights, strings of yellow and orange marigold flowers hanging on the entrance… As she looked up, her eyes fell on a board with, 'Laila Spa and Beauty Salon', written in gold.

Wow! Laila beauty parlor? Here…? It was a top end beauty salon that was part of five star hotels. She had seen its advertisements in magazines and often read interviews of the founder Laila. It was a nationally reputed beauty chain!

And now the spa is opening here in her locality!

She was suddenly reminded of Mohini who was their neighbor when she lived with her parents. Mohini was a supporting actress and lived alone in the opposite portion. On days when she had a shooting, a van would pick her up early in the morning and drop her back in the evening. She was very pleasant and behaved very courteously. She would give them guavas or cucumbers saying 'they were selling these very cheap near the outdoor shooting location. I got some for you'.

On days when she had no shooting, Mohini would go to the nearby parlor and get herself groomed. She would get her eyebrows threaded, her hair colored, and a facial done. Mohini wasn't very good looking, but looked very bright and glowing when she returned from the parlor.

Mohini had chuckled when she had praised her saying 'you look lovely' and added "'you are impressed with this… what would you say if I went to the Laila parlor? They just alter the person! It is a total makeover… It's magical… it may be expensive but worth every paisa. It's a beautiful experience… soft music, fragrant flowers, scented candles, beauticians speaking softly… two hours pass by in a flash. It's like a journey to heaven… they transform your face and your mind… they are true magicians…!"

She had been waiting to go to that parlor at least once and now the same famed Laila parlor was at her doorstep!

"What do you want, Madam?" The chemist asked… she told him what she wanted and then asked, "What is the occasion there? I can see a band playing…"

"They are inaugurating a beauty parlor. Actress Sumana is coming at ten O'clock. Madam, the road will be crowded with people in another half an hour."

She took the Cerelac tin from the Chemist, paid for it and came out to the street. A boy approached her and handed her a pamphlet he was distributing to everyone on the street. It was glossy and the pictures were elegant and eye-catching. The inaugural offer had attractive packages for facials, manicures, and pedicures. She herself never had any of these done. Mohini had said that the clipping of the toe-nails, the soaking of the feet in warm water, getting the feet massaged with cream and getting the nails painted was a soothing and relaxing experience. Though the desire had taken root then, the financial conditions in the family made it difficult for her to even think about it.

Her father was a primary school teacher. She had two older sisters and a younger brother. Her paternal grandmother too stayed with them and including her mother, the seven of them were fed from the meager teacher's salary. Despite their survival being difficult the silver lining was that every guest who visited their house had a common refrain, "Swaminatha… God may not have given you much, but he has given you three stunningly beautiful daughters who are like polished brass lamps; grooms will come and pick them just for their beauty… you have nothing to worry…" And that was true. As soon as her eldest sister completed her tenth standard, her paternal aunt insisted that she should get married to her son and got them married. Her maternal uncle chose her second sister as his daughter in law and thus both sisters ended up marrying within the extended family. Though they didn't ask for any dowry, her father still struggled to get the two daughters married in simple, traditional ceremonies. Seeing her father's condition, she decided, 'I will complete my graduation, do a computer course, join a good job and help Appa run the family. I will not get married in a hurry.'

She kept her word, studied hard and passed B. A. Economics with a First class. But when she found out that a computer course would cost anywhere between twenty to thirty thousand rupees and as she was wondering how she would manage, Vasudevan came home and introduced himself..

"My parents live in the village and my family is involved in agriculture. We have some land, and a house. I am the only son and am working as a Manager in 'Bharat Industries'. I earn a salary of thirty five thousand rupees. My father sold a small piece of land and gave me the money; I took a small loan and bought a small flat in Valasaravakam. I liked your daughter the moment I saw her want to marry her. You don't need to spend a rupee… we can have a simple temple wedding. You may give your daughter whatever you choose to… We have no demands whatsoever."

His straightforward and earnest speech, good looks, own flat in Chennai, a simple, affordable wedding… all this impressed everyone including her, and they consented for the marriage.

Soon afterwedding, she gently expressed her desires and aspirations to Vasu during their two day honeymoon in Yercaud.

"Is that all? No problem!" he said and as soon as they got settled in Chennai, he took her to a reputed computer training institute. Vasu chose a three month course costing fifteen thousand rupees. The course was to start in June and they offered her a discount of twenty percent since she had a first class in her graduation. They had to pay the fees on the first of the next month.

A day before the first, she began vomiting and her pregnancy was confirmed within the next ten days; which meant that they would have a baby close to their first wedding anniversary.

"I don't like this!" She said, not able to conceal her disappointment. Vasu consoled her as she wept softly, "There will be no change in your plans of doing the computer course or going for a job… it's just got postponed for a while, that is all. Once the baby is six months old, I will take care of the baby and you can do your course…"

That was a good idea. It was after all only a postponement; not a cancellation.

Baby Lavanya was born taking the best of both parents and was an adorably beautiful child. Vasu made sure that he took care of all the expenses of her delivery and didn't allow her father to spend anything.

"When my wife is giving me such a valuable gift, it is my duty to take care of the expenses, isn't it Mama?" Vasu had said with a chuckle.

The delivery charges, the expenses for the baby, the installments for the flat and bike, the EMI for the forty two inch TV he bought to fulfill her desire… and managing the monthly expenses is no less than a tightrope walk.

In a situation like this, the 'Laila beauty parlor' had surfaced and kindled her age-old desire.

She came back home, placed the vegetable basket in the kitchen, washed her hands and feet, fed the baby and cooked lunch. Once they finished lunch she handed Vasu the beauty parlor pamphlet.

"What is this?"

She stood patiently waiting for him to browse through it.

"Do you remember Mohini? I had mentioned to you about her. She had told me about this parlor and I have wanted to go to this parlor for a long time. They have opened a branch right here and are offering an inaugural package for three thousand rupees…"

Vasu stared at her wide-eyed.

"Why do you need a facial and all that? You are so naturally beautiful; like a goddess!"

He was in the habit of fondly calling her a goddess every time she dressed up well.

"No… I have been wanting to go to this parlor just once at least…"

The next day Vasu withdrew three thousand rupees from the ATM on his way back from the office and handed it to her saying, "I will take care of Lavi baby next Sunday… you go to the parlor and have a good time… enjoy yourself…"

Although heart of heart, she realized that a month's installment for the TV would be delayed; she couldn't contain her excitement and anticipation!

She woke up early that Sunday morning, cooked breakfast and lunch, and kept everything ready for the baby. When she left home at ten O'clock, there was a spring in her step as she came out.

It's been such a lifelong dream!

The security guard at the entrance of the parlor opened the door for her with a salute and a pleasant smile. As she stepped in, the beautiful ambience was spellbinding… the cool breeze from the AC fragrant with a floral scent, beautiful flowers in big vases, the walls filled with pictures of attractive Hollywood actresses and the well groomed beauticians dressed in smart skirts…

She walked up to the receptionist and mentioned her requirements.

"Have you taken an appointment?"

"No"

"There is a wedding party that has come in a group. All the exclusive facial rooms are full… even the manicure and pedicure chairs are occupied… you will have to wait for half an hour Mam…"

The receptionist said pleasantly, in impeccable English and smiled sweetly. She then guided her to a seat in the reception area and served her a glass of cold lemonade.

As she picked up a magazine from the side stand and flipped the pages, her gaze fell on the woman sitting on the opposite chair. She must be thirty or thirty five years old. She was a little stout and since she was reading with her head bent down, the bald patch with thinning hair on the top of her head was clearly visible.

A beautician walked out from the inner room with a couple of wigs in her hand. She came to that woman and made her try one wig after another and asked, 'Do you like this one? This…Or this…?"

The woman looked at her image in the mirror but didn't seem to be satisfied.

"My friend told me that these wigs will be very uncomfortable in the hot and humid Chennai weather. They make the head sweaty and itchy. She suggested that getting hair-weaving done would be better and a long term option."

"For that you need to speak to Arthi Madam, but she is busy with a client right now… please wait."

The woman went back to her magazine.

A few minutes later, a middle-aged woman and a twenty year old girl entered the parlor.

Mother and daughter…?

The young girl had thick hair growth on her upper lip and chin. Even her hands were full of dense hair… She could clearly hear what they were talking with the receptionist.

"They said the hair growth will reduce once we get waxing done… we have tried it several times, but it hasn't happened. It's grown back again within a month… she feels reluctant and shy to go to college…"

"Madam… threading and waxing will not work for such cases… laser treatment will be the best. If you get it done regularly for six months, the hair growth will surely come down. We can give you a guarantee. The skin specialist will be here soon. We can start the treatment once she gives the confirmation."

When she overheard the receptionist mention the charges for the laser treatment, she was shocked out of her wits.

But the mother was not shaken. "Don't worry about the cost… I want this problem to be solved… we have to get her married…"

As the mother and daughter went and sat on some chairs a little distance away, she turned her attention back to the magazine, but found it difficult to concentrate.

The lady who was getting her pedicure done got up and walked past her. The dark patches on her feet looked contrastingly even darker with the pink nail polish on her toe nails.

What was the need for the pedicure?

Her eyes fell on the posters on the walls.

"Are you overweight? Don't worry! Try our herbal steam bath for best results."

"Dark skin is no longer a problem. We can remove your old skin by 'Dermabrasion' and lighten your skin tone!"

There were pronouncements for the treatment of every possible problem!

No one came out of the exclusive rooms. How much more did she have to wait?

She forced herself to get back to reading the magazine.

Oh! An article by her favorite author!

"Want or Need?"

She found the title interesting and began reading…

"Many of us do not understand the difference between wants and needs. The things that are absolutely necessary for our survival, or those things that we can't live without are needs, while everything else is a desire, a wish, a want.

Air, food, shelter, clothes, education, health, exercise and anything related to them are necessary for survival and we work hard to ensure we have access to them. But the rest of the activities like eating out, going for movies, buying every piece of jewelry or attire that catches the eye are certainly wants and we can definitely live our lives without them. Borrowing money and getting into debt just to fulfill our wants is a sure recipe for disaster. Hence, we should stop for a moment before we do anything and ask ourselves, 'Is this really necessary? Is this a need or a want? Once we ask this question and truthfully answer it; we will be able to understand that most of the activities we do and things we accumulate are only wants and not needs."

She read the article once and then reread it. It felt as if a little bubble had burst in her heart.

She put the magazine down and got up.

"It will take only five minutes Madam," said the receptionist courteously.

She just mumbled, 'It is getting late' and walked out.

As the doorbell rang, Vasu came to the door carrying Lavanya and opened the door. He was surprised to see her and asked, "What happened? Was the parlor closed? How come you are back so soon?"

She came inside quietly, took out the three thousand rupees from her purse and said handing the money to Vasu, "The parlor was open but I didn't feel like getting anything done."

"Why? This has been your desire! You had wanted to do this for so long!"

She didn't answer immediately but stepped forward and hugged her husband and child together.

"Yes, I wanted to… But it is only a want, not a need! She said and buried her head in his shoulders.

2020

Savages

Athai, father's sister, sat on the swing with her left leg folded and her right leg pushing the swing gently.

Handloom saree, white blouse, Rudraksh string around her neck, a smear of sacred ash on her forehead, her gray hair tied in a high bun…

Her eyes were, as usual, focused on the vast expanse of sky visible from the window.

"Athai… I am Kamali… look at me, I arrived here from America just two days ago. Even Lavanya and my husband have come with me to India. Look at Lavanya; everyone says she resembles you a lot!"

Kamali said again, nudging Lavanya towards her aunt, "Athai see…" She turned Lavanya's face towards her Athai and said,

"Lavanya, this is your grandma, my Athai… she is the one who brought me up. When I was your age, I would refuse to leave her lap. She would tell such beautiful stories, you know? I would sit on her lap and pester her to tell stories…" Lavanya hesitated and clung to her mother, refusing to go to Athai.

Athai gently turned her gaze and without a change in her expression, placed her hand on Lavanya's head. She turned her gaze back to the sky outside.

Kamali had expected Athai to hug Lavanya excitedly, but she was stunned to see her cold reaction. She looked at her elder sister Poorni dazedly.

"What is the matter, Poorni… Did Athai even understand what I said?"

"Yes, it looks like she did from the way she placed her hand on the child's head. She has been like this for the past six months. She first stopped lighting the lamp for the Gods in the pooja room and saying her prayers. When I asked her why, she said, 'I have done enough… it is now your turn to do all this.'"

"In the last two months, she has stopped speaking… she would answer in monosyllables initially, but now even that has stopped and she has gone completely silent."

"What is the doctor saying?"

"She is physically healthy… but lost in her own imaginary world! Age is catching up… The doctor says let her be the way she wants to… Once I help her bathe, get dressed and make her sit on the swing, she is here the whole day. She eats her meals on time and we help her to go to the bathroom several times during the day. Whenever she gets tired of sitting, she lies on the swing to rest her back. Her movements are very restricted and she hardly walks.

The doctor says that this is common among aged people and that hers could be a case of senile dementia…"

"Dementia? Do you mean short term memory loss?" "Well… he is not sure, Kamali."

"Athai has always been the quiet type, but her condition wasn't this bad when I came two years ago. You didn't tell me about her ailment when I spoke to you a few days ago?"

"I could have told you if she was ill or something. What could I possibly tell you about her condition? I do feel sad seeing her in this state but it isn't much of a problem… she is just lost in her own world."

Kamali was saddened listening to what she heard; she went close to Athai and caressed her lovingly. "Athai, I came here wanting to talk to you… but you don't say anything…"

Kamali looked up, grabbed her sister's hand, and said in a choked voice, "You and your husband take care of Athai like she is your own mother!"

"Why wouldn't we? Didn't Athai look after us from our childhood till we got married? Following our Amma's untimely demise; it was Athai who took her place and brought us up like her own daughters. Now that she is unwell, isn't it fair that we take care of her Kamali?"

"I am so far away and not able to contribute in any way…"

"How does it matter, Kamali? I am here and am able to do it. You too would have done the same or even more if you had been here! Now, forget all that and sit here. You have traveled all the way from America; why don't you stay with us for a month? I felt very sad when you said you have to leave in fifteen days."

"Yes Poorni… Raghu is doing an important project and it is very difficult for him to take off even for this short time. Since his sister's son is getting married, we certainly have to attend it. I have somehow managed to make it. The wedding is next Friday and I have to leave the following Sunday. I too have joined a new job just recently and couldn't manage to get more than two weeks leave."

Poorni stroked her younger sister's head affectionately.

"There are still eight days left for the wedding. Why don't you come and stay with us for four days in between? We will get to spend time with Lavanya dear…"

Poorni had two sons and she always longed to have a daughter. Kamali realized that her sister desired to fulfill that longing by spending some time with Lavanya. Kamali looked at Poorni pleadingly and said,

"I too want to stay here so badly, but it looks difficult Poorni… You know that Lord Murugan is the family deity for my mother-in-law's family, don't you? Last year when Raghu underwent an open heart surgery, we had taken a sacred vow to visit all the six Padai Veedu temples of the Lord once my husband gets well. Raghu and I are leaving by car tomorrow and plan to visit all the six temples within three days. We don't want Lavanya to get exposed to the harsh sun and are leaving her behind with my mother in law."

"Why don't you leave Lavanya with us, Kamali? Let me be with her for at least three days?"

Kamali bent forward and hugged her sister.

"Poorni… please… since my mother in law stays with us in the US for six months every year, Lavanya has grown very close to her grandmother. She is ready to stay with her happily even in our absence. Apart from that, they have a stay-home Bihari cook, a driver and all other comforts. My mother in law's brother's grandson Ashok too stays with her and is doing his graduation studies. He says he will take Lavi to different places and have a lot of fun for those three days. He has already made all the plans. That being the case, if I say that I want to leave Lavi with my sister, it won't look nice. I hope you understand Poorni."

Kamali's disappointment was evident in her tone.

"That is alright… but you have to stay with us for at least two days before you leave. I will not listen to any excuses.

OK, come on, let's go and have something to eat. Vedam Mami will give Athai her snacks and take care of her."

As the two women walked in, Athai's thoughts traveled back in time through her fuzzy memories.

How old was she? Four?

Her father was a lawyer and their house was always abuzz and lively with visitors and clients. They had servants for all the household chores.

Murugan was the cook, a fair, good looking thirty five year old man with well-oiled and cropped hair. He was an amazing cook and was ever smiling, pleasant and was everyone's favorite.

One night it was raining heavily and the electricity had snapped. All the rooms were lit with candles. She was sleepy and when she was pestering her mother to tell her a story; Murugan picked her up saying, 'come I will tell you a story...' and put her to bed. It was pitch dark. He started telling a story she had never heard before and grabbed her attention. Taking advantage of the darkness, he touched different parts of her body and made her fondle him. Engrossed in the story, she too didn't pay heed to the touch. Suddenly she felt a slimy fluid between her fingers and a deep stench. The end of the story and the jerking of the hands coincided and Murugan wiped her hand with his lungi. "'If you don't tell this to anyone, I will tell you a longer story tomorrow." He whispered.

She could smell the stench while brushing her teeth and during her meals the next morning.

Thankfully, for some reason, Amma did not send her to bed with Murugan in the following days. Despite being too young to understand what was happening, she did feel a sense of peace being away from Murugan and she forgot the incident soon enough.

She was seven years old… and went to school by car everyday with her mother accompanying her. Her mother would come and pick her up from school every evening.

One day Amma had a high fever and couldn't come to pick her up from school. The driver alone had come with the car. "Shall we go to the beach, baby?"' he asked and veered the car towards the beach. She loved playing in the sea water, but Amma hated it and would always say, "don't get wet like this, you will get a fever" and stopped her from playing in the water. That evening, he allowed her to play in the water to her heart's content.

As it began to get a little dark, he bought her an ice cream and drove the car to an isolated spot. "Your dress is so wet here…it is dripping", he said and touched her inappropriately. When she whimpered, "I want to go home," he said, "if you behave like a good girl, I will bring you to the beach often and buy you ice cream" and started doing all kinds of things with her. She was in severe pain. When she started crying, he threatened her saying, "if you tell anyone, I will never bring you to the beach again", and started the car.

She developed a fever the same night. Her father was enraged by the fact that not only had the driver taken her to the beach without permission; he had also allowed her to play in the water. He refused to listen to the driver when he said that "it was she who had insisted on going to the beach," and fired him from the job immediately.

She was eight and it was vacation time.

It was an unusually quiet afternoon with no visitors. All the elders had finished lunch and were enjoying their afternoon siesta. She was bored and sat alone on the swing when Guru, who was related to her father and stayed with them, came in. He had completed his graduation and was working in some company.

She asked, "Don't you have work Mama?"

He said, "I have a headache and have taken leave for the day. Isn't anyone at home?"

"Amma and Appa have gone to Kanchipuram for some condolence; Mami and Chithi are sleeping inside." She replied. He screwed his eyes without stopping the swing and thought for a while.

He looked at her and said, "I have bought some imported nail polish.... Come with me... I will polish your finger and toe nails for you." She followed him excitedly to his bedroom on the first floor. He closed the door behind him and said, "I will apply the nail polish if you keep quiet," while taking out the nail polish bottle from the almirah. "I have been waiting for this opportunity for so long," he murmured as he applied the nail polish on her toenails and fingernails.

"Lie down without moving your hands and legs... otherwise it will get smudged," he said and holding her tight with one hand, he lay down over her. 'I want to go', she insisted and then pleaded feebly 'Let me go'. He cupped his palms over her mouth. She was breathless and her stomach churned.

"If you make a sound or create a fuss, I will wring your neck and kill you!" He threatened and then continued menacingly,

"If you dare say anything to the elders, I will tell them that you are the one who is a dirty girl and that you peep at me when I am changing my clothes or taking a bath. That will make things really difficult for you, remember that!" She was in tremendous pain and wanted to cry aloud and panic gripped her. She jerked herself up and ran out crying, 'let me go… let me go…'

She would wake up with a start at night and her stomach would feel queasy. She felt miserable for several nights after that incident. She would want to wail uncontrollably and felt terrified, but didn't know who to talk to and would cry silently, burying her face into her pillow.

She turned eighteen.

She had got married and it was her wedding night. She was feeling an inexpressible nervousness and anxiety all evening. As she walked into the bedecked bedroom with a jug containing milk, her hands trembled and her palms were sweaty.

Her husband disregarded her uneasiness, embraced her forcefully, and kissed her hard on her lips. Her lips bled and she panted for breath. He overpowered her and in a few moments…the same sliminess, the same stench pervaded her senses. She didn't know what to do!

Aa… aa… She screamed loudly and fell unconscious like a log of wood. Not only that day, it was the same story for the following few weeks as well. A month from her wedding, her in-laws wrote to her father saying, 'Your daughter is abnormal; she is mentally sick' and packed her off to her parents' home for good.

From that day on, her mother and father became her world. It was her brother, his family, and especially his two daughters who took center stage in her life later on.

"Athai, I am leaving. I will come back and stay with you after four days, Ok?"

Kamali hugged Athai while Poorni said disappointedly, "Why don't you leave Lavanya with us? You just don't listen to me."

"I told you Poorni. There are a lot of people at my in-laws' place. They have a cook and a driver; even Ashok is there. I am sure they will take good care of Lavi. Don't worry. I will come back from my trip and surely stay with you for a day. Can I leave now?"

Before she could turn and take two steps away

Athai suddenly grabbed Kamali's hand anxiously…

"No… Don't… they are savages… they will tear your child to pieces! Her life will be ruined!"

She said softly but clearly!

2015

Just One Word

Vedagiri stood stunned, not being able to believe the words he had just heard,

"Don't joke Ranganathan."

"What is so funny about this? I came here only because your son in law sent me."

Vedagiri controlled his anxiety with effort and eyed the person sitting opposite him with suspicion.

"Wh… what did he ask you to tell me?"

Ranganathan smiled.

"He is ready to come back to your daughter."

Vedagiri sat speechless for a few seconds and said 'Don't joke' in a pleading voice.

Ranganathan said, rising from his chair, "why don't you trust me Sir? Should I go and tell Sundaram that your father in law refused to believe me!"

"Oh! No no… please don't get annoyed. I have been waiting desperately to hear these words for the past three years; that is why I was a little shaken. Please sit down… Is my son in law really ready to accept and live with Selvi again? Please tell me this is true!"

"Why would I come unless Sundaram sent me here with his message? He told me last night, 'You take my car, go to my in-law's place and tell my father in law that I have consented to live with Selvi again'… See for yourself Sir, Isn't that your son in law's car parked there?"

When Vedagiri turned his gaze outside the window, he could see the black car he had given as dowry; Vedagiri heaved a sigh of relief realizing what Ranganathan was saying was indeed true. Lord Murugan had finally heard his prayers.

Had his son in law really gotten out of his obsession for that dancer?

Vedagiri had brought up his only child with love and affection. By God's grace, she will no longer have to live with the shameful tag of being 'abandoned' or 'discarded'.

Vedagiri was moved to tears and his palms became sweaty.

"But… there is one more thing…" Ranganathan began hesitatingly.

"Sundaram feels that no one should know that it was he who came forward and sent me here… and hence…"

"And so…?"

"You must come to the city and request Sundaram saying, 'Let bygones be bygones… please forget what happened and accept Selvi. You both are young and do you think it is right for the two of you to live separately like this'?"

"If you appeal to him… Sundaram himself will come here on an auspicious day… Do you understand?"

Of course Vedagiri understood.

The same Sundaram had disregarded Vedagiri's appeals and requests the other day, and pronounced that the dancer was more important in his life and walked away. Today, Sundaram feels that it would be beneath his dignity to come forward and is requesting his father in law to come and beg before him… Isn't that what it is?

Vedagiri's jaws became clenched and his nostrils flared with anger at how flippantly and poorly Sundaram treated relationships and people… .but that rage lasted only for a few seconds.

Is my self-respect more important than my daughter's peaceful life?

The moment this question rose in Vedagiri's mind, he mellowed down and steadied himself.

What is wrong with what Ranganathan is saying?

Whatever said and done, Sundaram is a man; his son in law. It is absolutely justified if he thinks that his father in law should come and make a formal request. Isn't that the tradition too?"

"Sir, any problem…?"

"No, not at all… You are saying that I should go there and invite my son in law. Aren't you? I have no problem with that. All that matters to me is my daughter Selvi's happiness. She should not shed tears anymore. I will come… tomorrow itself."

"I will now take your leave." Said Ranganathan, getting up to go.

"Wait a minute son, you have come here like lord Hanuman and given me a ray of hope. I cannot let you leave like this. You must have lunch and go."

"No thank you. I don't have time. I had promised Sundaram that I will be back before it gets dark. He will be waiting for me."

"In that case, I won't stop you. Let us not do anything that makes him angry!"

"Hey! Boy, come here. Go and get a bundle of sugarcane, a bag of peanuts, raw bananas, pumpkins and twenty coconuts from the backyard and put them in the boot of the car. I cannot let my guest go empty handed! Please wait for a minute, son..."

Vedagiri went in and came out soon with a tray bearing betel leaves, betel nuts, a gold bordered dhoti, a towel, and a ten-gram gold coin.

"What is all this, Sir?"

"Oh, this is nothing! You have brought me news that I have been waiting for with bated breath. Please accept this as a small token of my gratitude. We will have a grand celebration when my son in law visits us..."

Once Ranganathan left with his car and hands full of gifts, Vedagiri walked back into the house briskly, calling out to his wife 'Navaneetha... Navaneethaa...', the tears he had been holding back for so long streamed down his cheeks.

Vedagiri was born into a well to do family with massive lands, cowsheds full of cows, trunk loads of cash, jewelry... he still continues to live a charmed life with the blessings of Goddess Lakshmi. He has no worries and lives a life of bliss, but that incident happened and hit him like a bolt from the blue three years ago.

Vedagiri and Navaneetham were blessed with four children but the last child Selvi was the only one who survived. She was the apple of her father's eye, his pet.

Selvi was not only the sole inheritor of all his wealth and assets; she was also blessed with good looks, modesty and graceful behavior. She was among the best known and most adored girls in town.

Vedagiri realized that his daughter was interested in studies and going against his family tradition, he allowed her to complete her high school education. He searched hard for almost three years and finally found Sundaram as the ideal suitor for Selvi.

People in town still spoke for hours about Selvi's wedding, and admired its grandeur and elegance...

Streets covered with colorful canopies, scores of musicians, music bands... an orchestra performance in the evening... sarees and dhoties for anyone and everyone... four days of meals for everyone in town...

Sundaram was a husband worthy of Selvi in every way-be it good looks, status or wealth, but the only thing he lacked was character. When Vedagiri was making enquiries around town about Sundaram before the wedding, he had heard murmurs about Sundaram's habits not being very clean...

Sundaram belonged to an esteemed family; he was educated, cultured and had no dearth for wealth and comforts.

But...?

"He is a young man with raging hormones; he will surely calm down once he settles into marriage..." People around Vedagiri advised him and suggested that he shouldn't lose such a good alliance for trivial reasons. Vedagiri agreed and got his darling daughter married to Sundaram in a grand wedding ceremony.

Everything was fine for the first two months, but gradually problems cropped up and things took an ugly turn. Within a year of marriage Sundaram bluntly declared, "I don't like you and cannot live with you any longer." Selvi had returned to her father's place labeled as a 'discarded woman' and it was only today that her fortunes had finally smiled on her.

Vedagiri sat on the swing musing with Navaneetham seated opposite him.

Selvi was inside.

"This was something I had been hearing for the past couple of days but never expected it to get sorted out so fast. Arumugam had told me that the dancer had become associated with some other man from Singapore and was neglecting Sundaram."

Arumugam had also said, "Don't worry… your son in law will come back very soon. His muse has lost interest in him and has moved to newer pastures."

"I didn't believe him at that time and I thought he was saying all that only to keep my hopes alive… but the Goddess has finally opened her eyes…"

"Where is our son in law now? Is he living with his parents?" Navaneetham asked.

"No… I made discreet enquiries from Ranganathan and have come to know that Sundaram is living in a hotel room in the city. Don't you remember that Selvi's in-laws have strictly asked Sundaram not to step into their house without Selvi? That is why Sundaram stayed back in the city."

"You must go and invite him back here before he changes his mind and goes back to that cursed woman. God has been kind. I have found peace after years! I don't know what sin we had committed because of which our child had to suffer so much! We must forget everything like a bad dream… Please go to the astrologer and find an auspicious day for our son in law to come here. Also, go and meet him with your uncle and aunt, and request him saying, 'You must be large hearted and come to our house. You must forgive Selvi and accept her...' Inform him about the auspicious day as well..." Navaneetham spoke with a mix of smiles and tears and suddenly walked into the puja room and prostrated before God. "Muruga! You have ended my misery!" She cried and prayed aloud.

The following Friday was supposed to be the most auspicious day according to the astrologer. He said it was the best day for people who had separated to come together and start a new life. Vedagiri left with a few elders in the family with trays of betel leaves and fruits to welcome his son in law. As soon as the news spread around, droves of women came running and crowded around Navaneetham asking curiously,

"Navaneetham, is it true? Is your son in law coming back?"

"Selvi's patience and devotion have finally paid off!"

"Navaneetha, do arrange for a special puja at the Mariamman temple on Friday morning."

"Make sure to ward off the evil eye using an ash gourd..."

"Where is Selvi? She is nowhere to be seen?"

"She must be sitting and daydreaming in happiness..."

The women chirped happily and drowned Navaneetham with suggestions and advice.

The moment Vedagiri returned from the city with the good news about Sundaram having agreed; the household erupted with joy and it looked like it was wedding time!

"We must meet Selvi's in-laws tomorrow, give them the good news and invite them here on Friday. There are only four days left. Navaneetham, get the room on the first floor cleaned and ask Kandappan to white wash the room. Buy all the groceries needed and make sure that there is at least one sweet and a lot of savories for every meal. We must serve the best food possible. And since there is no time to get new jewelry made, we will go to the town on the way to Selvi's in-laws' place and buy a gold chain for our son in law and a pearl necklace for Selvi. What do you say, Navaneetha?"

While Vedagiri, Navaneetham and others went about excitedly planning the events for Friday, the main protagonist Selvi sat in her usual place calmly as if she had nothing to do with anything that was happening around her.

"Selvi must be feeling shy; she must be brimming with happiness at the prospect of meeting her husband…"

Selvi had no reaction to all such statements flying all around her. She just went up to her room, sat by the window and looked out at the garden. As she sat there gazing out of the window, the six months of marital life she had spent with Sundaram three years ago flashed before her eyes.

It was just four days since their wedding.

Sevi was shocked when she went up to call Sundaram for lunch.

Sundaram sat with a bottle with a yellowish brown liquid and a glass in his hand.

Though no one in her family had drinking habits, Selvi had seen men drinking in movies and read a lot about it in papers and magazines. She was a little shaken by what she saw.

"What is this?"

"What?"

"What are you holding in your hands?

"Oh! It feels wonderful to have a peg just before meals. You know, even doctors say that it is good for health and we should have it like a tonic! Why don't you have some Selvi?"

Within a week, Sundaram's friends began coming home and they would sit and drink together regularly. Selvi was getting really worried and she told Sundaram,

"Please stop this. It doesn't look nice with your parents down stairs. It is so disrespectful…"

Sundaram turned a deaf ear to Selvi's plea, smiled and walked back to his friends with a new bottle in hand.

"We thought things would change once he gets married; but it doesn't seem to have worked. He is back to his old ways. Why don't you try to talk to him dear?" Sundaram's parents had pleaded with Selvi with tearful eyes. That was when it struck Selvi that this was not something new but a long standing vice. All Selvi could do was shed tears of helplessness along with her mother in law.

Her husband's character and habits became clear to Selvi within a month of their wedding.

I, me, myself… my peace, my happiness… was all that mattered to Sundaram.

He cared a damn about his parents, his wife, and what happened to them.

He would be drunk half the time and wouldn't have his meals on time. He would create a ruckus, scream and shout when he was sloshed. He picked fights with everyone at home and walked out with his friends.

On those rare days when he was sober, the torture would be of a different kind altogether.

"Come here…" He would call out to Selvi.

The moment she went close to him, he would look at her with disdain and annoyance.

"What is this saree you are wearing? It looks like a bed sheet. You just don't know how to dress elegantly… Get out of this right now and wear the saree and blouse I got you from Chennai…"

She had worn those sarees and blouses a couple of times just to please him.

Sleeveless blouses and see through, transparent chiffon sarees…

He wouldn't stop at that.

"Wear this lipstick… let your saree slip from your shoulder like this… turn around… bend forward… walk…. look at me…"

Sevi hesitated to look at herself in the mirror with her waist, hips and breasts revealed seductively through the transparent saree.

He would get angry when she refused to go out with him dressed like that.

"Why can't you come dressed like this? What is your problem?"

"Please don't force me to come in front of your friends dressed like this. Chee!… I hate the way they stare at me!"

"What is wrong if they see you? Why do you think God has blessed women with beautiful, sexy bodies? It's for men to see and appreciate…!"

He would tease her and annoy her insensitively without caring for her feelings and her hesitation. He would clap his hands and laugh aloud callously seeing her discomfort.

One day…

He returned from Chennai with a large packet in hand.

When she entered her bedroom that night, he handed her the packet saying, 'wear these right now'.

When she opened the packet….

A night dress as thin as an onion peel with matching bra and panties….

"Wh… what is all this?"

Don't be ridiculous and make me angry… go, wear these and come back here."

"I feel shy. Please No!"

"Why should you feel shy? Am I not your husband? If you don't wear such clothes at eighteen, when will you wear them? Come on, don't argue unnecessarily. Can't you see I have brought them for you with so much love?"

As usual, Selvi gave in that night as well.

Selvi tried consoling herself saying, 'After all he is my husband. Being his wife, it is my duty to keep him happy and fulfill his needs.'

When she came out wearing the sexy nightdress, Sundaram made her bend forward, walk, lie down, turn around and said looking at her lustfully, "You know which dress this is? In one of the movies, the actress Rathna dances to a song wearing this outfit. I was blown away seeing her on screen and I begged her to give me the outfit as a token of my admiration for her! Keep it carefully. Let me see if you can become a little more sexy and romantic by wearing it." He said lasciviously; laughing heartily.

Selvi was shattered seeing his vulgarity and cheap taste.

How can a man compare his wife to a cheap dancer and force her to wear the dancer's clothes? How disgusting!

Is there no difference between me and that woman who strips for money?

Even though she felt enraged, Selvi went about her daily life without revealing her feelings, while Sundaram continued to torture her more and more with every passing day.

"Why won't you wear this dress? Are you shy? Why should you feel shy? I will believe you if you say it doesn't suit your ugly face… but…"

"Whatever said and done, there is no one like Rathna! So dainty, so elegant! Her gait, her stance, her look… everything is so perfect! Look at you! You look like a buffalo!"

"You dare ask me why I haven't come home for a week. Why should I? All I get to see at home is your morose face and my perpetually irritated parents! I am just fed up. Just feel happy that I am here today."

"Oh get lost! I am a man and will go to a hundred women if I choose to. Who are you to question me? Am I using your father's money; Hell no! I am spending my own money. Just shut up or go away…"

He abused Selvi constantly and one fine day he fought with his father, took his share of the family assets and went away to live with Rathna.

Sundaram's father vented out his frustration and shouted at his son when he was leaving,

"You… rascal… how can you even think of leaving your wonderful wife and living with that whore? Oh my God! Do you think this is justified in any way? Sundaram, beware of a woman's curse! It can destroy you. Just give that slut whatever you want to, and come back home… do you even realize… it's you today… tomorrow it will be someone else for that woman? I can't bear to see all this… what is wrong with my daughter in law? She is a gem of a girl… please think again before you take any step…"

Sundaram stood smoking and laughing callously with his friend Rangathan as his father screamed and shouted. He then sneered condescendingly and said,

"You ask me what is wrong with her, Appa? Tell me one thing that is good about her! You just tied a village bumpkin around my neck and want me to live with her. No way! I cannot live with her… not in this life! It is fruitless to cast pearls before a swine… How will you know Rathna's worth? I am going to live with Rathna in Chennai henceforth."

Sundaram's mother caught hold of her son's collar and cried helplessly,

"Don't do this… you rogue! Don't ruin this young girl's life…"

Sundaram jerked her hands away and moved back without saying a word.

"Son, I beg you…. just meet Selvi once before you go… she is a priceless, young, eighteen year old girl… please…" His mother pleaded tearfully.

Sundaram said glaring at his mother,

"Don't waste my time Amma. Let me tell you something just before I leave. All this wealth and assets are those which my grandfather has left behind and I am the legal inheritor.

I will send someone for money whenever I need it. Make sure you send the money… do you understand?"

Those arrogant words made his father flare up.

"Wh… what did you say? Do you think your father is an idiot? I have already given you your share. You will not get a single paisa more. You can step into this house again only if you accept my wonderful daughter in law Selvi. Don't forget that, you scoundrel!"

Sundaram shrugged his shoulders and walked down the steps, but he suddenly stopped, turned around and said mockingly with a wicked smirk,

"Appa you keep repeating that Selvi is so wonderful and such a perfect daughter in law… and you constantly lament saying Selvi's life is destroyed and that she is an innocent lamb…Let me tell you something; you are not that old yet… you are not even fifty… Why don't you keep her as your mistress and take care of her…? Amma too is getting old…I am sure you know what I am hinting at, don't you?"

Sundaram said wickedly and rushed into the waiting car before his stunned father could raise his hands to slap him.

Selvi went back to her parents' house the very same day.

In the last three years, Selvi hadn't stepped out of her parents' house even when her father or other relatives went to plead with Sundaram or when she heard about the untimely death of her mother in law. She didn't say a word or express her feelings when people gossiped about her saying she had withered ever since her husband walked away or when they said that she had been unable to take the humiliation. They would judge her and at the same time sympathize with her; but Selvi didn't speak a word.

Selvi thought hard for two days and came to a decision. It was Thursday morning and she realized that she could not wait any longer. Selvi went in search of her father and stood in front of him.

Vedagiri, who was engrossed in showing his relatives the new clothes and the gold chain he had bought for his son in law, was surprised to see Selvi.

Selvi had never come anywhere near a place where there were visitors or men. Vedagiri was amazed to see her stand by the door of the living room.

He asked, "What is the matter, Selvi?"

Selvi replied softly, "I need to talk to you, Appa."

"What?

"Ok, Tell me." Vedagiri said surprised.

"…"

"What is it dear? Do you think we need to buy some other things for our son in law? Do you want us to do something grand for him? Please tell me freely… don't hesitate dear. All this is for you."

Selvi hesitated and then said almost in a whisper, "Appa, can we go to the first floor? I want to talk to you alone."

Maybe the new beds in the bedroom on the first floor are not good enough… she must be feeling shy to speak in front of outsiders… Vedagiri wondered as he got up.

"Of Course! Let us go."

Vedagiri walked up the stairs followed by his daughter.

He asked Kandappan, who was hanging new curtains in the bedroom, to step out.

Vedagiri looked at Selvi affectionately and asked, "What is it, Selvi dear? Tell me…"

Selvi wet her lips and began to speak slowly.

"Appa, don't feel sad listening to what I have to tell you. You know I am not one who says things in anger or does anything impulsively."

"What is it Selvi? Why are you building this preamble?"

"It is a serious issue Appa… please listen to me patiently… I am sure you will understand me."

"Come to the point, Selvi."

"Appa, please understand… I do not want to go and live with him."

"Wh… what?"

"Yes Appa… please stop all these arrangements right away. Send them a message asking them not to come here."

"Why? What happened?"

"Relax Appa… For the past two days I have been waiting for you to ask me if the decision you have taken is acceptable to me. But…"

"Selvi… I… I thought…"

Vedagiri sat on the bed dazed. He held his head in his hands.

Selvi spoke after a minute's silence.

"Appa, I am going to tell you in detail what I haven't told anyone in the last three years. I was not devastated because he left me and walked away with that dancer… it was the kind of things he said, his actions and his behavior that shattered me to pieces… He would force me to wear indecent, revealing clothes and ask me to dance like that dancer Rathna. He would compare me with other actresses and say, 'you don't have thighs like Nandini; a slender waist like Nalina; breasts like Geeta….'" Her voice choked as she continued further.

"He would describe the sensual experiences he had had with other women in graphic detail… he made me squirm like a worm… he had no issues with his friends leching at me or even touching me! He would scold me saying 'what is wrong with that!' Appa I tolerated everything, but the day he was leaving, what he said to his father really crushed me. When my father in law was arguing for my sake, he said to his father in the presence of his mother, 'Appa, Please feel free to keep Selvi as your mistress… I have no objection.' That was the last straw and…."

Selvi was unable to finish and began to cry softly…

Vedagiri couldn't bear it anymore and he cried aloud,

"Stop it Selvi… stop!"

"Why… why did you suffer all this torture alone… if you had just said one word… just one word earlier…"

Selvi said wiping her tears,

"I am saying it now Appa… NO! I don't want to live with him anymore. I am not ready to accept a man, who not only doesn't know how to love his wife, but also refuses to respect her and her feelings as a human being."

"Appa, I am happy staying here with you and Amma. Appa, please allow me to study further… consider me your son… Appa, please…!"

Vedagiri stared unblinkingly at his daughter who spoke with a mix of anticipation and fear.

He slowly walked down the stairs without saying a word in response. He stood in the middle of the living room and called loudly, "Is anyone there? Go and call the accountant Shanmugam..."

"He had mentioned that he had fixed his daughter's wedding and was worried about the expenses for the jewelry and the wedding trousseau..."

"I want to tell him not to worry about the money and jewelry. He can take this gold chain with the tiger-nail pendant, silk dhotis and silk sarees and conduct his daughter's wedding in style with our blessings... Just go and bring Shanmugam here immediately..."

As Vedagiri ordered the servant to fetch Shanmugam... his aggrieved, but concerned words echoed in every corner of the house.

1984

TRUST

She opened the door and stood outside.

The streets were isolated and empty. There were no school children, no postmen, no vegetable vendors… not a soul was in sight!

What kind of place is this?

She felt vexed as she walked to the gate and craned her neck to look to her left and right. There was not a single window open in any of the houses on the other side of the street.

"The summer in this place is killing… once people shut their doors at eight in the morning, they open them only after eight in the evening… otherwise the hot breeze can be unbearable. There are dust storms that blow once in a while. If you open the doors or windows by mistake, everything in your house will be covered in a thick layer of dust and it is a back breaking task to clean the house! You have a small child… better to be careful…"

She was reminded of the words Murugesan had said when he had come to the railway station to welcome them once she reached there with her husband a week ago. Murugesan was one of the other Tamils employed in her husband's factory.

She slowly walked back into the house and shut the door. She picked up the magazine lying on the stool and read it from cover to cover. Only a few Tamil magazines were available here. She was used to watching TV, going for plays and reading a variety of Tamil books and magazines in Chennai and found it difficult to pass her time in this small town in North India. In fact, it was not even a town; it was just a colony with thirty to forty houses built for the employees of the factory. There were three rows of houses in the colony and the officers, like her husband, lived in the first row… they were eight buildings with four flats each, two on the ground floor and two on the first with thirty two flats in all. A Bengali family lived next to her flat and there were two Hindi families on the first floor.

She had gone to their houses and introduced herself the day they reached there. Since she wasn't fluent in Hindi, she found it difficult to talk to any of them for more than ten minutes and the interaction with them got restricted to them asking 'How are you… How is your baby…?' courteously. She would just smile in response.

She raised her hands above her head and yawned. Should I take a short nap?

She could hardly sleep at night because of her infant son crying continuously. She invariably woke up red eyed and tired.

The moment she wound up with all her chores and saw off her husband to work, her baby would wake up and kill all her chances of catching even a few winks of sleep. She would have to carry him constantly to keep him quiet.

When she was in Chennai, her mother had got him used to being carried all the time by keeping him on her lap and now the baby expected the same here as well. Was it even possible?!

The water supply stopped by eight in the morning and she had to fill up water in the buckets and pans and also get breakfast ready for her husband before that. She had to take care of the baby and keep lunch ready by twelve thirty when her husband came home for lunch. She would finish lunch, clean up the kitchen, wash the vessels and the clothes....

It wasn't as if her husband was unaware of her difficulties. He had put in a word to the neighbors to help them find a good maid as soon as they had moved in. The standard response they got was that it was very difficult to find good house help in that small town.

She got up with a start, listening to the baby cry. She changed his soiled nappy and fed him sitting on the bed. By the time she wiped the baby clean, put baby powder, changed his clothes and freshened up, it was five O'clock in the evening.

By the grace of God, her husband came home with some good news that evening.

There was a lady known to the peon in his office. She lived in a village a kilometer away and was ready to come in for work around nine in the morning and stay on till five in the evening. She would help with all the housework and cooking. They had to pay her a thousand rupees plus food. As per the decision, she arrived sharp at O'clock the next morning.

As she opened the door, she was stunned to see the lady standing at the door.

This lady?... A maid?

She was hardly twenty two years old. She wore a flashy, trendy nylon saree, with a deep necked blouse. She had her hair tied in two plaits and her toenails and fingernails were painted. She was not only beautiful but was stylish and fashionable as well. Was she going to work as a maid?

Rameswari smiled, understanding her reaction. She said, 'move' and walked into the house. She completed all the housework and cooking fast without taking a moment's break. The chapatis were soft and the vegetable gravy was delicious.

The spotlessly washed clothes were folded and kept in the almirah. The glistening vessels went to their places in the kitchen and the house was swept and mopped clean without a speck of dust to be seen.

Her work was remarkable indeed and she seemed extremely efficient.

She left at four thirty in the evening saying, "I am leaving early today. From tomorrow, I will stay till Sahib returns from office."

The moment Rameswari left, the ladies from the first floor came down and asked, "Have you kept Rameswari for house work?"

She was surprised to see that they already knew her maid's name. She just nodded with a smile.

"People here have a saying that 'households that turtles and Rameswari enter into, get ruined'. You are new here.... you don't know... we thought it was our duty to warn you and that is why we came running..."

As she blinked, not understanding much of what they were saying, one of the neighbors continued, "Rameswari is a useless ass... a characterless woman! When Rameswari was working in the Marketing Manager Mr. Dasgupta's house, she tried to seduce him and was driven away. It was the same story when she worked in a house in the town. You are a young woman and your husband is also young... Don't get into trouble unnecessarily. Send her away tomorrow morning itself. Look at her face, her makeup and style! Chee… a real slut!"

The two women said what they had to and went back home.

Was Rameswari a loose woman?

It was true that she was far more beautiful, well dressed and fashionable than what was expected of an ordinary maid.

But…

She didn't mention anything about all that to her husband when he returned from work that evening, but she asked Rameswari directly the next morning,

"Rameswari, the ladies from the first floor were saying all kinds of things about you. What happened in the Marketing Manager Mr. Dasgupta's house? Tell me."

Rameswari slumped down against the wall and her eyes welled up with tears. She started to speak with a sob,

"We poor people should not be born beautiful… especially women like me who have no option but to work as housemaids. We cannot be good looking… wear stylish clothes or talk pleasantly with a smile! I am aware of everything. You might be wondering why I dress up so well and keep myself well groomed despite knowing everything… My husband is a gem of a man and has managed to earn a lot working as a truck driver.

"Last year both his legs went lame in a road accident and he is now restricted to the house. He not only has lost his self-esteem and confidence but he constantly berates himself saying, 'I have caused you so much suffering when you should be living comfortably…' I dress up well, smile and behave jovially just to make him feel that I am happy and have no complaints. I behave exactly the way I did before his accident. I am certain that he would have taken excellent care of me had something similar happened to me! I am doing the same thing now. Isn't it my duty to do so? Does a husband and wife relationship mean only physical pleasure? Isn't it about sharing and standing shoulder to shoulder in good times and bad? I will not hesitate to do whatever it takes to give my husband some peace and solace! Why should I care about society? People will be jealous if one lives well and clap their hands in glee when one is in trouble! Society is not at all important for me! Amma, I am telling the truth… it was Mr. Dasgupta who misbehaved with me and when I refused him, he turned the tables and accused me instead. It was the same story with the house in the town. A poor, underprivileged woman should not be born good looking. Amma, I don't know how many trials and tribulations I have to face before I manage to make my husband mentally and physically strong like before…"

As she looked intently at Rameswari who was crying inconsolably, she was reminded of an incident that happened to her soon after her marriage when she was working in Chennai.

One day she was late coming back home from work in the evening. She had stayed longer than usual to complete some urgent work and her manager Bhaskar dropped her home that day. As she ascended the steps to her house, she stopped on her tracks hearing her father in law's angry voice,

"You will not listen to me, will you? Do you know that people are gossiping about her and Bhaskar in the office? I had told you that the head clerk had mentioned this to me ten days ago. But do you even care? See, the time is eight O'clock and he is dropping her at our doorstep at this late hour! How dare they behave so shamelessly! Will you be a man and put her in her place or … should I…?"

She stood rooted as she cringed and her ears burnt like fire. She then heard her husband speak firmly without allowing his father to continue.

"You want your daughter in law to work, you want the money she earns, but you will not trust her! Is that what you are saying Appa? No woman will be able to live peacefully with her husband while there are men like you who gossip and lead irresponsible lives! I am a MAN and that is why I trust my wife unconditionally. I have been quiet all along because you are my father. If you dare say anything like this once more, I don't know what I will do! I know my wife well and she lives and behaves the way I like her to! Mutual understanding and trust is paramount between human beings… remember that!"

That night she had not spoken a word and lay with her head resting on his chest thinking, What kind of a man is he? Isn't this true masculinity? She remembered being overwhelmed and unable to sleep.

It was so true…

Without trust… There could be no individual, no family, no relationships, no humanity, and no society!

Mutual trust is extremely vital between humans.

As she looked at Rameswari with compassion and said, "Get up and wash your face. Have a cup of tea and get on with your work Rameswari…" the tone of her voice clearly seemed to say, 'Don't bother about anyone, I trust you fully…'

1982

AIYO! I AM SCARED...

Neither the tall Eucalyptus trees reaching for the sky, the green carpets of thick tea plantations, the azure blue sky with white fluffy clouds nor the multitude of colorful butterflies could catch her attention.

She is standing with her head resting gently on the window. Her trademark smile and mischief are missing from her face.

Her eyes searching for something in the infinite, turn towards her husband asleep inside the room. His eyes are shut; she isn't sure whether he was actually asleep or just lying exhausted. In any case she continues to stand by the window silently not wanting to disturb him.

He has to be really unwell otherwise was this a body that could lie listlessly like this?

She turns to look at the well-built man once again.

She is reminded of the first time she met the tall hunk with his strong and muscular arms.

She was a college student then and had gone to watch the college cricket tournament on the insistence of her friend. Among all the players on the field, it was the wicket keeper behind the stumps that caught her attention!

'Wow! What a physique!' She had marveled aloud.

"He is known as the Samson of the University'. Don't you know?" Her friend's question had got etched in her memory.

Three years passed by. It was almost a year and a half ago that she met him a week after she joined the Connemara public library as an assistant librarian.

"Will you please note down the names of these books. I have to go urgently." He had said without raising his head and looked up only when he neared the desk. "Oh Sorry, Isn't Murugan Sir there?" he asked, raising his eyebrows quizzically.

"I didn't notice you, thought it was him." He said sheepishly.

The next time he came, it was almost one O'clock in the afternoon. "Would you like to come for a cup of coffee?" He had offered and she had gone along.

That was when she told him about seeing him on the cricket field when he was in college.

"God! What a fantastic memory you have! I regret not meeting you then and wasting three wonderful years of my life." She loved the way he had said mischievously.

Frequent meetings followed.

He mentioned that he had planned to study further post his graduation but his father's sudden demise had forced him to drop those plans and take care of the family tea estate.

She told him about her parents and her sister a year younger to her.

He spoke to her at length about his life in the tea estate and she told him about her love for the serene hills and a calm life.

Then... well...

They got married on an auspicious day the very next month. As she lay with her head on his enormous, taut shoulders, he had said, "'Our house is very isolated, darling… there are no other houses around… Of course, there are the workers' quarters a short distance away and we have the cook and driver staying in the servant quarters here. The nearest town is 18 miles away and we have to travel that far even for basic needs. Will this kind of life scare you or bore you?"

She thought silently for a few minutes and had replied, "You will be there, won't you? That is enough for me." She said with a sense of pride.

In the early days of their family life, he had hugged her tight and asked her if she was scared of the howling of the jackals at night.

Her voice dripped with admiration and pride when she said, "How can you even think of asking me this question with me in your arms? How can any fear come near me with this powerful body to protect me?"

The sun slowly begins to disappear behind the hills and a blanket of darkness spreads over the landscape. She looks at him yet again…

She had to stay back with her parents for over fifteen days when she visited them for her sister's wedding. He had come a day before the wedding and returned the very next day. An hour before he had to leave for the railway station, when they were alone in their room on the first floor…

"I too will come with you darling… the wedding is over…do you have any idea how much I have pined for you in the last few days?" She had said burying her head on his broad chest and muscular arms.

He lifted her face up with his palms, "I missed you too sweetheart..."

"Then shall I come with you?" She asked excitedly.

"'I would love that! But, don't you have to stay here to help your mother? Your sister is leaving for her honeymoon tonight...won't it be difficult if you too leave today? It will be better if you stay back for a week and assist your mother with winding up everything."

This was their first separation since they got married a year ago. It was tough... but it was true that her presence will be very useful for her mother. The very thought of being away from him tormented her immensely.

"Ok! You seem to be keen to leave me alone and go! Be alone and lonely in that jungle... I bet you are going to call me back saying you miss me and beg me to come back soon!"

He returned to the estate alone that evening.

It was sixteen days by the time she could complete all the post wedding work, close the financial dealings and leave.

He was waiting at the station to pick her up.

She could spot him even before the train wound its way into the station.

How could one miss that tall, herculean man!

But, she could mark a change the moment she neared him!

"What is the matter dear?"

"Nothing, How are you? You said you couldn't bear to be away from me for a moment and... you've been away for sixteen days without sparing a thought for me! Naughty girl… just wait and see what I will do…" he said forgetting that they were at the railway station and slipped his hand behind her waist.

His hand felt warm and his eyes looked slightly pale and yellow. His face was a little drawn.

The moment they got into the car, he pulled her close saying "welcome home my dear."

"Have you seen yourself in the mirror lately?"

"Why, haven't I shaved properly?" He asked mischievously, caressing his chin.

"You don't look alright… your eyes look yellow. Why, what is the matter?"

"Mm…"

She asked once again seriously, "Tell me, are you alright?"

"Why? Have I lost weight? Come close to me darling. Why are you so far away from me?" He said impishly.

They crossed orange orchards, miles and miles of tea plantations and drove through winding roads, turning around sharp hair pin bends as they traversed the eighteen-mile distance. Though he stopped the car multiple times, teased her mischievously and seductively, something rankled her mind constantly.

Her suspicions were proven right the moment they reached home.

The cook told her that he hadn't eaten well for the past ten days and was running a fever for the last two days. He even had a couple of bouts of vomiting! Since he had a lot of work, he hadn't gone to the doctor!

All he could do was smile sweetly listening to the cook spill the beans.

"Why will someone go to the doctor eighteen miles away just for some light fever and vomiting? Why are you so worried dear?"

She wasn't convinced.

They went to the doctor the same day with the driver driving their car.

"You have come to see me when the jaundice has really become severe! Why this delay…?" The doctor reprimanded them and admitted him to the nursing home immediately.

She stayed with him in the hospital for the next two weeks. The driver would travel eighteen miles back and forth to get them food and other necessities from home.

While discharging him from the hospital, the doctor had said, "Jaundice is not something to be afraid of, but can be fatal if it becomes serious. Thankfully your husband is strong and healthy; otherwise it could have been a problem."

He added, "I asked you to stay in hospital till he recovers completely only because you stay far away in the estate. He is much better now, and I am allowing him to leave because he says he has a lot of work to do… But both of you listen, you have to consume bland and simple food for three or four weeks and… please be disciplined", the doctor said playfully.

On their way back, she said, "I thought, only I have eyes for your sexy, strong body, but the doctor too…" Both of them had laughed aloud.

That was certainly true!

Despite being unwell for almost four weeks, he hadn't lost weight and his rippling muscles remain intact.

She walks to her husband and places her palm on his forehead…. it feels hot.

He turns around to her side, feeling her touch, and opens his eyes. They are unusually red.

"What is it darling?"

He tries to smile… but coughs instead.

She bends and places the basin under his face.

He vomits a stream of thin, yellow liquid.

She is petrified and asks, "Shall I call the doctor?"

This is the umpteenth time she had asked the question in the last few hours; and this time he nods in agreement.

She helps him lie down and calls the doctor on the phone from the other room.

"Doctor, he has been feeling unwell since morning. He says he has a severe stomach ache and is vomiting yellow fluid…"

The Doctor shouts without allowing her to finish, "What is this? What is the reason?"

She hesitates a little.

"He had some drinks last night, Doctor." She says softly.

"I can't believe this!" The doctor says grinding his teeth. "Didn't I tell you to avoid a normal life and be careful? Ok, I have to see him immediately. I have given my car for service. Can you send your car to pick me up?"

She says Ok, rings the bell to call the driver and asks him to hurry up and leave.

It's three thirty in the afternoon.

She finds the stillness of the house and the calm outside irksome.

The cook, who hadn't gone home for many weeks, went on leave for two days just yesterday.

Confident that he had recovered completely, her husband had pleaded the previous evening, "Can I have a small drink?" She had refused in the beginning.

"Please…"

He had implored like a child and she had relented. But he had not stopped at one and had three instead.

The thirst of several weeks of separation got the better of them and he hugged her passionately.

"No darling…"

"Please dear, I am alright… please!" He begged and she gave in, melting into his inviting body.

He was running a high fever the moment he woke up the next morning.

"Look at this dear! Didn't I say no?"

"It's nothing… Don't worry about these small things and make a fuss," he said, pushing her away.

But, by ten O'clock, he started having severe stomach ache and cramps.

Repeated vomiting…

Even though he felt really weak, he refused to call the doctor. He had consented only now.

She walks into her husband's room… he beckons her with his bloodshot eyes.

Persistent coughing…

Even before she can bend and place the basin… he rests on her shoulder and vomits blood.

What is happening?

Her heart is racing and her mind is agitated…

He slumps on the bed as if he is unconscious…

She runs to the phone to call the doctor.

"The doctor has just left, Madam."

She runs back to him.

When she bends to look at him closely… she notices a change…

The broad chest, the bulging shoulders… are motionless and still…

She feels a chill spread over her…

She touches his shoulder and whispers, "darling…"

He doesn't move… the half open eyes remain stuck upwards…

She shakes him disconcertedly…

No movement at all…

Her agitation increases as the gravity of the situation sinks in…

She runs out frantically and whispers to herself, "doctor, please come fast."

Then she stands at the door and calls out, "Somebody, please come…!"

Tears begin to flow steadily…

Her husband lies inside that room. "With this strong, muscular body with me, why should I feel afraid?" The body that she had marveled and admired is still there; the broad rocklike chest, those sinewy arms are all there…

But? But?

She is scared…

"Aiyo! I am scared! Someone please come! I am afraid to be alone with… this body!" she screams and then begins to cry aloud…

1981

Muthamma

A shadow appeared in front of me. I put my pen down and looked up.

Muthamma…

Wizened face… A large red bindi on her forehead… Well-oiled hair pulled back and tied in a tight bun. A grimy, yellow Thali thread around her neck… Silver bracelets on her hands, anklets and toe rings hands in her feet… Her mouth full of betel leaf and tobacco juice. Her protruding stomach hanging low…

"Uff…. my God…" She sat down slowly struggling to carry her own weight.

I have known this woman for more than ten years now. She was working as a maid in our house when we moved to this town.

I think she and I would be roughly of the same age.

"How old are you Muthu?"

"Who knows? I may be as old as six donkeys!" She would say in jest whenever I asked her that question.

When I came here as a twenty year old newlywed; Muthamma already had two children aged two and four. Her husband Velayudan worked in a factory in a town nearby. He earned four thousand rupees a month plus bonus. They led a reasonably comfortable life.

I need to mention something exclusively about Muthamma at this juncture.

She was a perfectionist and her work was impeccable. Her sweeping and swapping, cleaning the utensils, washing clothes, everything was flawless. There would not be a speck of dust on the floor or the windows, no grease on the pots and pans! Not a chance!

Want to get murukku flour pounded? Have to go to the flour mill? She was ready to do everything! She worked almost through her entire third pregnancy and ensured that she completed all the work even on the day of her delivery. Eight days after her delivery, she said, "I cannot come for work anymore. My husband says, 'just stay home and take care of your health and the children. Why should you go out to work and suffer so much…?"

Her eyes shone with the satisfaction and happiness of knowing how much her husband cared for her.

After that, she would visit us once in a while with her infant daughter Jyothi and sit in the backyard. She would proudly show the silver anklets her husband had bought for their daughter and the gold nose pin he had bought for her with his bonus money.

When Jyothi was around eight months old, Muthamma looked a little plump. I asked her with suspicion.

"You are getting your periods regularly, aren't you Muthu?"

She just lowered her head shyly.

"Muthu?"

"It's three months, Amma."

Her infant was eight months old and this woman was already three months pregnant! What was happening!

Won't the older child be malnourished and neglected?

I spoke with a trace of annoyance.

"You have two healthy sons and a cute daughter… Instead of focusing on educating them and giving them a good life; what is this stupidity Muthu? Shouldn't you think about your children and be a little more careful?"

"Just because this one is on the way, do you think we will starve the older ones and not buy them clothes to wear? What are you saying, Amma?"

"Is keeping them fed and clothed enough? Isn't education necessary for them to come up in life? How old is your eldest son now? Six? Do you even intend to send him to school? He will be able to earn well only if he studies, won't he?"

Muthamma clapped her hands and laughed aloud.

"What big education has my husband got, Amma? Isn't he earning well? Even my children will grow up well like their father. Don't you think one needs to be blessed to have lots of children?"

The discussion ended there.

What can you talk to someone who was like a horse with blinkers; not ready to see or accept anything?

Six months after the fourth child was born, Muthu underwent a miscarriage. The very next year she was carrying again! Not being able to see her so anemic and pale, I asked her bluntly disregarding her annoyance.

"Are you expecting again, Muthu? You keep complaining and crying constantly about not feeling well and then you get pregnant almost every year! When will you have the opportunity to build your health? Will you listen to me? Go to the hospital in town and see the lady doctor. Your pregnancy is still in the early stages… and I am sure the doctor will tell you what to do… it can be handled easily, there is nothing to worry…"

Muthamma looked at me incredulously.

"What are you saying, Amma?"

"Don't you understand Muthu? This will be your fifth child… and you've had a miscarriage as well. Go to the lady doctor; get an abortion and a family planning operation done. It is for your own good… and for your family…"

Muthamma didn't allow me to finish and covered her mouth with her palms. She then closed her ears in shock, not wanting to listen to what I had to say.

"How could you even think like this? Aren't you a mother too? Do you realize what you are saying? Children are God's boon! Who are we to refuse them?"

"God has already given you four boons! Why do you want a fifth?"

"Ha! That is what you feel! It is a sin to refuse God's will."

"What sin are you talking about? Didn't we stop at two children? Isn't it better not to have children instead of struggling to bring them up and making them suffer in the bargain?"

"Our children are our assets. Who will take care of us if we fall sick? You shouldn't forget that Amma! You keep harping about struggle… What struggle is it? Children are born and grow up on their own. What is the problem for us?"

Her ignorance made me laugh.

"Children are born naturally and grow up on their own? What nonsense is that Muthu? Aren't we parents responsible for bringing them up? The way things are and prices are skyrocketing, people are struggling and toiling hard to bring up even two children and give them a comfortable life! Do you even realize that?"

"No, Amma, just stop it. The God above us who plants the saplings will certainly water them too! We villagers cannot be stone hearted like you city dwellers…. Let destiny take its own course…"

In the following years, Muthamma suffered one more miscarriage.

In the meantime, Velayudan fell into bad company and took to the bottle. He spent most of his earnings on alcohol and they found it difficult to make ends meet. Muthamma sold whatever little jewelry they owned, took a loan, bought two cows, and began selling milk. I was her most regular customer.

I bought two liters of milk every morning and evening. She would often complain about not having enough money to buy cattle feed for the cows. She would cut grass from our lawns to feed her cows.

Surprisingly, there was a gap of two years and now she was carrying her sixth child. As I looked at her intently, a wave of anger rose within me.

Muthamma who was healthy and fine had become frail.

Married at fifteen; a mother of six before she was thirty… three children lost, and carrying the next! The woman who lived with her head held high, decked in gold jewelry, now looked like an old hag-weak and fragile!

"Muthu, how come you are here at such an odd hour?" You look tired and listless. Is your back hurting? Shall I get you some hot coffee?"

Not getting any response from her, I went into the kitchen and returned with a glass of coffee.

"Here, take this."

She sipped the coffee slowly, got up and washed the glass and handed it to me.

"The cows are hungry. Can you lend me 100 rupees?"

"Why? Didn't you send them for grazing?"

"Malayan is out of town. He has gone to my brother's place. Ezhumalai is running a fever. He refused to go out in the sun…"

"Did you say Ezhumalai has a fever? I saw him in the cinema theater last evening?"

She just bowed her head without saying a word.

Muthamma's eldest son Malayan was seventeen and the second son Ezhumalai was fifteen, but both had grown up to be utterly worthless boys. They neither studied nor did they pick up any vocational skills. They just wasted their time smoking bidis, watching movies and listening to cinema music. Once in a while they would take the cows out for grazing, that is all!

"Don't mind me saying this Muthu… your sons seem to be wayward and treading on the wrong path… .Even my husband was very upset a few days ago… why don't you reprimand them and keep them under control?"

Muthamma said with a deep sigh.

"They are young and playful Amma. It is common for boys of this age to be playful and irresponsible. I am sure they will be alright when they grow up. Why should we break our heads now?"

She mumbled something in justification and walked away with the money.

She delivered the following week. The umbilical cord hadn't separated properly and she suffered a lot of bleeding. Her sons Malayan and Ezhumalai delivered milk in her place.

The milk was extremely watery and I sent the gardener to enquire. He came back and said that the two boys were selling half the milk to tea shops without their mother's knowledge and adding water to the rest of the milk. He also mentioned about Malayan being not even eighteen yet, insisting on marrying his maternal uncle's daughter. Ezhumalai was throwing a tantrum about buying a T-shirt similar to the one his favorite film star wore for eight hundred rupees for Diwali. He told me about Jyothi being down with severe diarrhea. Velayudan was coming home drunk and creating a ruckus every day and Muthamma cried helplessly. My heart felt heavy listening to Muthamma's woes.

As I sat lamenting for four days, about how a family that could have lived happily and comfortably was suffering because of ignorance, I got the news that couldn't have been worse.

Velayudan had consumed arrack as usual on an empty stomach and was returning home in an inebriated condition when a speeding truck lost control and crushed him to death. The truck driver had driven away and disappeared using the darkness of the night to his advantage. Velayudan's story had ended abruptly the same night.

Velayudan's coworkers at the factory and his friends took him on his last journey with beating drums, crackers bursting and flowers being showered on him. They buried him with pomp and show and soon forgot all about him

Within the next two months, Muthamma's family was literally on the streets. Her husband's untimely death and the incessant bleeding following her delivery sucked all the energy out of her and she was devastated. The eldest son Malayan went away to permanently stay with his uncle. Ezhumalai got lured by someone who promised to get him a chance in the movies. He sold one of the cows at a throw away price overnight and ran away from home to Chennai with the money, starry eyed, with dreams of making it big in the Tamil film industry.

The adolescent daughter Jyothi came knocking at my door and cried inconsolably, narrating the tragic situation in her house.

"Amma, the relatives came to perform the last rites of my father, stayed for ten days and finished all the rice and millets we had. We haven't received any money from the company either. We have nothing to eat. My mother is sick and I don't know how to milk the cow. My little brothers are too young to understand what is happening and cry continuously. What will I do Amma…?"

I spoke to my husband, and gave Jyothi a thousand rupees and some tablets for fever.

"Take this and buy all the groceries you need for ten days. First make sure that you all eat well. Ask Amma to have this tablet with some tea. Buy her some bread if you can… Ask her to come and see me once she is a little better…"

Jyothi walked away sniffling, wiping her tears.

I came in and sat down. My stomach churned thinking about Muthamma, her family and her misery. I felt helpless and frustrated thinking about how to make these people understand! I picked up a magazine lying nearby and began flipping the pages in an attempt to keep my helplessness and agony at bay.

1980

Jaya Jaya Shankara

Iswar woke up with a start at around five in the morning. He was sweating badly.

His eyes fell on the lifeless AC fixed to the window. He was annoyed.

He had paid thirteen thousand rupees to buy it, but what a waste! The frequent power cuts made life miserable.

After slogging it out the whole day, one couldn't even have a good night's sleep!

He turned to look at his wife sleeping next to him.

He noticed that she was fast asleep. How could she sleep so soundly?

After having lived in centrally cooled houses in America and being used to all the luxuries, how was she able to adapt so easily?

Iswar was sure he couldn't sleep any longer. He came to the balcony and lit a cigarette. He sat on the rocking chair and smoked quietly

Iswar, Dr. Iswar was an expert in Psychiatry.

After completing his MBBS, his fascination for America drew him there for higher studies. He finished his medical education and started his Psychiatry practice. Within a few years he had made a name for himself and began earning extremely well.

Dr. Iswar came to India on a trip, got married to Nithya and returned to America with her.

Iswar's earnings increased manifold owing to his brilliance and courteous behavior. They were soon able to buy their own, comfortable home. They had two cars and all the luxuries. They visited India once every two years.

Janani was born four years after their marriage; and Gayatri, two years later.

Both were adorable!

All was well till Janani turned ten. But problems started soon after.

One evening, after Iswar had finished dinner and was watching TV; Nithya came to him with a serious face and said,

"I want to talk to you, Iswar."

Iswar nodded, not taking his eyes off the Miami Miss World pageant being telecast live on TV.

"Shut off the TV. I want to talk about something important…"

What was the problem?

Iswar switched off the TV worriedly.

"I think we should go back to India…"

"You mean for holidays?"

"No… not for holidays… but for good."

"What?"

Nithya could understand his shock.

"Please… you must listen to me patiently. I have been thinking about this for quite some time now. I feel we will face a lot of problems here once the girls grow up. Janani will be a teenager in a couple of years. We have to think of all the things that will happen once she grows up. Dating and going out with boys is very common here. Adult girls and boys can go out with each other and do whatever they want. They can date anyone they wish and decide to not marry that person and start going out with someone else… all this is acceptable here. The question is, will we be able to take it if our daughters do the same? How far can we allow them to go? Where do we draw the line? I don't think I can be at peace with Janani going out and doing as she pleases. Whatever said and done, our culture and traditions are different. Also, Janani has started asking me a lot of questions lately, and I am unable to answer her convincingly. She is a growing child and naturally has a lot of questions. I have a feeling that she will soon be influenced by her peers and her attitude might change. And if we bring them up according to our traditions, they might develop a complex of being different, isn't it? Why should we go through all those problems? Having given a thought to all the aspects, I feel settling in India is be the right thing to do…"

Iswar didn't respond for a long time. He sat deep in thought.

"Iswar? Why don't you say something? What do you feel?"

"I am thinking, Nithya. What you say is right but will I have this kind of practice and earn so much in India?"

"Haven't we earned enough already? Don't you think our children's future is more important?"

"Nithya, it's not only about the money. What about comforts? What about my job satisfaction?"

"I have thought about that too. Can't we build our own nursing home in Madras with the money we have? Why can't you continue your practice there? Please Iswar… think about the children…"

Nithya won.

It was ten months since they sold their house, cars and everything in America and returned to India. They bought a beautiful house in Nungambakkam. Instead of wasting time looking for land to build their own clinic; Iswar joined a private hospital and started his practice.

Despite that, the amount of trouble they had to face to get the gas connection, the permissions, and permits for the house construction activities from the municipality, the struggle for school admissions for the girls…. it was a real nightmare!

In the last ten months that he had spent in India, Iswar had got vexed and disgusted with everything.

My intelligence and skills are getting wasted…

We don't have even a quarter of the comforts we had in America…

What am I going to achieve with these traditions and culture?

It is better that we just dump everything and go back to America….

Iswar was angry, frustrated, and annoyed.

As the cigarette butt scalded his finger, Iswar shrugged his hand.

"What are you doing sitting in the balcony so early in the morning?"

It was Nithya.

Iswar said in a soft voice,

"I am fed up with the whole thing, Nithya… Shall we go back to the US?"

Nithya pulled a chair and sat close to him.

"Why? What happened so suddenly?"

"This is not a knee jerk reaction, Nithya. I don't like anything here. People don't know the importance of time. They don't appreciate hard work. They don't seem to do anything properly. All you see is lethargy, laziness… There is a shortage of everything… Oh God! Why can't these people understand the simple fact that to have a comfortable life and earn money, you need to work hard?"

Nithya laughed.

"Is life only about comforts and money?"

"Then what else? Tell me Nithya."

Nithya smiled and said,

"No, you are not in a good mood right now… Let me get you a hot cup of coffee."

She came back in ten minutes with steaming hot coffee.

Iswar had the coffee and lay down for about half an hour. He felt better.

As he got ready and got into the car to leave for the hospital, Nithya leaned into the car window and said,

"Can you take half a day off tomorrow and ask Dr. Aswath to see your patients? I want you to come with me."

"Where?"

"Shankaracharya (The Saint and religious head) has come to Ponnamallee. Uncle told me that he may leave for Bombay via Bangalore directly from there. He may not visit

Madras for two more years. I thought we could go and seek his blessings…"

"Why do you want me to come, Nithya? Why don't you take the car and go with the girls?"

"Please…"

Iswar couldn't refuse and he agreed.

The next morning they woke up at four in the morning, bathed, got ready and left with uncle, aunty and the girls.

The Benz car they had bought from the US refused to start and they were forced to take the Fiat.

The six of them somehow managed to stuff themselves in the car and left.

"This cage-like car costs fifty thousand rupees! And there is a long waiting period to even get this car… Unbelievable! What a country!"

Nithya didn't reply to Iswar's grumbling.

It was six thirty by the time they entered Poonamallee and reached the venue. The Saint had gone to visit a temple in the neighboring village. They would have to wait for some time.

Two days of continuous rains had made the ground wet and slushy.

Iswar lost his patience within two minutes of waiting there.

Let's leave!

Just when the thought rose in his mind, he heard the distinct chant.

"Jaya Jaya Shankara…"

"Hara Hara Shankara…"

As the chorus of chants came closer and became louder, it reverberated like the holy Om chant.

A crowd was approaching them from a distance…

"Jaya Jaya Shankara…"

"Hara Hara Shankara…"

The Pontiff, attired in his ochre clothes, walked in the middle of the crowd with his staff in hand. A smile played on his lips.

"Jaya Jaya Shankara…"

"Hara Hara Shankara…"

The Pontiff's feet splashed in the muddy rain water and his wet ochre clothes clung to his body owing to the drizzle. However the smile on his face was intact.

"Jaya Jaya Shankara…"

"Hara Hara Shankara…"

Iswar who stood disinterestedly till then suddenly felt as if Saint's gaze had fallen on him for a few seconds. He hurriedly kicked his footwear away and folded his hands humbly.

When the Saint walked past Iswar, he stopped for a moment. His smile was like a lotus in full bloom and he continued to walk forward.

The special full moon or Paurnami pooja started within half an hour. The Pontiff performed the pooja for five long hours sitting in one position, without even having a sip of water while Vedic chants like the Rudram and Chamakam reverberated all around.

By the time the pooja ended and everyone received the holy water, it was three O' clock. The Saint personally offered the holy water to every single person in the crowd with a benign smile on his face.

When Iswar walked up at the end of the line and politely held out his hand, Mama came forward and introduced Iswar to the Pontiff.

Offering Iswar the holy water, the Saint looked into his eyes intently and uttered 'Narayana, Narayana'… his usual way of blessing everyone.

A few minutes after the Saint went inside, as they were standing among a crowd of people who were waiting for a personal audience with the Saint, one of his assistants came out asking, "Who is Dr. Iswar? The Saint is calling him inside."

Iswar and his family went inside.

It was a middle sized room with the Pontiff sitting on a deer skin on the floor on one side. Once all of them prostrated before him, he gestured to them to be seated on the other side of the room.

One by one, people waiting outside began coming inside to take the Saint's blessings.

"I am Rajarathnam Pillai from Salem… my only daughter is unable to speak. Please bless her, O Holiness."

The Saint placed a little sacred ash and vermillion with holy rice on a small piece of banana leaf and handed it to the man saying, "Don't worry, all will be well."

Another man accompanied by his daughter prostrated before the Pontiff, and said in a choking voice, "My daughter has got engaged and the groom's family is ready for the marriage without demanding anything as dowry... but I don't have money even to buy the wedding saree. I don't know how I will manage..." The man started sobbing and couldn't finish what he was saying.

The Saint called one of his well to do devotees standing nearby,

"You told me that you are going to celebrate your sixtieth birthday next month and asked for my blessings for conducting it in a meaningful way. Why don't you celebrate a charity wedding along with yours and take the load of this poor father?" The Pontiff said, pointing to the man who had requested for help earlier. The well to do devotee agreed happily and the man and his daughter left with relief and gratitude.

Similarly, a boy who had no means to continue his education found a way.

A mother who was helpless and couldn't manage to bring up her children found a solution when her sons were admitted into the Veda pathashala or school run by the monastery.

A man, who claimed that he had lost interest in family life and wanted to become an ascetic, was advised saying, "first take care of all your responsibilities. We will decide about this later."

These and so many other such cases... The Pontiff had something for everyone.

Not a morsel of food for more than six hours and yet completely involved in his divine duties...

He seemed to be a living example for the Sanskrit verse 'Sarve jana sukhino bhavantu' which means 'May all live happily'...

He walked barefoot in the slush, got drenched in the rain, traveled miles in the heat… all for the service and well-being of humanity… what was all this effort for? What made him dedicate his life for others?

What kind of a heart and mind was this?

Can there be anyone like this in the world?

The Saint, who hadn't looked at Iswar till then suddenly turned his sharp gaze towards him and smiled.

'You were questioning and complaining about what this country has and what kind of people we are… Do you understand now…?' His smile seemed to ask…

Iswar felt as if he had been struck hard by a whip. His whole body shivered and went cold.

Money, wealth, and comforts cannot add any meaning to life, can they?

Does happiness lie in having the right thoughts with the right values?

Is bliss inside me and is it up to me to look for it?

Iswar stood up with a start.

"Jaya Jaya Shankara…"

"Hara Hara Shankara…"

He chanted softly and prostrated before Saint.

The tears from his eyes dropped onto the floor.

1978

She died On Friday Night

The smoke from the wet logs hit her face as she bent down to stir the rice porridge simmering on the wood fire. Her eyes burnt when she tried to hold her nose and blow hard on the logs, trying to make them burn better.

Her eyes brimmed with tears, not being able to take the heat from the logs and the pain in her stomach. Her heart felt heavy and she wanted to cry aloud but she controlled her sobs because she didn't want her husband Visvam, who was sleeping in one corner of the same room, to wake up. She lifted her arm and wiped her eyes with her blouse sleeve and slanted her head to look at her husband.

She felt a wave of sorrow rise in her as she watched her once healthy, well built husband, who worked hard to earn for the family, lie weakly and helplessly. She quickly turned her face away.

She wondered who could have cast an evil eye on her happy family. Who could have thought ill about their simple family that went about life happily and with dignity, despite their meager earnings and modest living conditions?

The porridge was ready. She took the vessel off the fire, cooled the porridge, and poured it into a glass. Since there was no milk, she added a pinch of salt and some buttermilk. She walked up to her husband with the glass and called out, "get up, I have got porridge for you. Please have it and go back to sleep if you want to."

Visvam sat up and asked,

"Did the children have anything? What did you eat?"

"There was some food brought from the lawyer's house. The children had that and are playing outside. I am not hungry and don't feel like eating anything. I have to go to Saroja's house to make Murukkus. I will have a few of them. You have the porridge…"

Tears streamed down Viswam's eyes as he had the porridge and handed back the glass to her.

"What is this? Why are you behaving like a small child?"

Viswam wiped his tears, and holding Rajam's hands, he said with a sob, "Rajam I have become useless… you and the kids are forced to be at other peoples' mercy… I don't like it at all…"

"Please… don't say such things… You should give me courage. What will I do if you lose hope? Isn't it a blessing that despite losing your legs, you are still there for us? I don't ask for anything more. The Goddess will always be with us and take care of us… don't worry…"

What was the Goddess going to do! Everything was already lost.

Nothing could be done. -

It was not as if she was not aware of how dire the situation was. She had to say such things to keep her devastated husband's morale high.

Rajam had lost her parents very early in life. Although the Goddess had not blessed her with the love of a family; she did bless her with a noble character and arresting looks.

One of the aunts who brought her up till she turned ten, sent her to do odd jobs at a doctor's house. Rajam started by running errands for the doctor's children and the elders in the family but soon graduated to being their most favored cook. She was only nineteen then.

The doctor couple was kind-hearted and felt that it was their moral responsibility to provide a secure future for the loyal and hardworking Rajam. They began looking for a suitable alliance for her and their eyes fell on Vedachalam, the owner of the 'Brahmin Coffee hotel'. Vedachalam's only son Viswam had completed his SSLC and was working in his father's hotel. He was twenty two.

Viswam and Rajam got married on an auspicious day.

Within a few days of her marriage, Rajam had got a measure of what kind of a man her father in law was.

She realized that the widower Vedachalam hesitated to remarry because of his grown up son, but desired the companionship of a wife desperately. Every time Rajam went to give him coffee or water, he would make it a point to feel her hands; he would stroke her head or try to hold her hands in the excuse of seeing her henna. He would say he has a headache and ask her to massage his head. He would stare at her breasts as she bent down to massage his head. He tried a lot of other cheap tricks as well.

Rajam, who had never known a father's love found nothing wrong with Vedachalam's behavior initially, but she soon realized that this wasn't fatherly love but lust!

She wondered how she could stop it.

"Do you know how much my father likes you? Yesterday I heard him telling his friend Sambu, 'I always missed having a daughter, but Rajam has fulfilled my desire.' I felt so happy." Viswam would say.

"Today is Friday and I forgot to buy flowers, but Appa gave me these after finishing his evening prayers in the hotel saying, 'Viswa, give these to Rajam'."

What could Rajam tell her husband who was blissfully unaware of what was happening?

Vedachalam was a shrewd man indeed.

Vedachalam would never ask Rajam to massage his head or press his feet in Viswam's presence. He would do such things only on the days when he left the hotel under Viswam's care and came home early.

Once she understood Vedachalam's true intentions, Rajam would get the neighbor's kids to her place the moment she spotted Vedachalam approaching home. Or, she would hurriedly lock the house and go away to the market or the temple to avoid him.

Afraid that problems could crop up between father and son if she said anything; Rajam naively kept her mouth shut. She tried hard to avoid getting caught alone with her father in law as far as possible.

But, how long could this hide and seek last?

She was six months pregnant with her first child within eight months of her wedding.

One day after Viswam had left for the hotel, Vedachalam stayed back saying he was feeling a little giddy. But, within ten minutes, Viswam came back home because he had forgotten the keys of the cash box.

Rajam had just come out of her bath and was wearing her saree in the kitchen. Viswam caught his father peeping through the closed door, leching at Rajam.

Viswam proved himself to be a real Man. He managed to rent a small room on rent in another part of the town the same evening, and walked out of the house with his wife and their belongings, without saying a word to his father.

Vedachalam too didn't find it necessary to ask for the reason. Rajam also didn't say a word.

All three of them seemed to know the answer anyway.

Viswam bought the essential items for the house with the money he had and with Rajam's help, began to sell masala vadas, steamed and spiced chickpeas (Sundal) and murukkus on the beach. Since the items were tasty and of good quality, they sold like hot cakes and they were able to earn enough to run their life comfortably. Although, he couldn't provide his wife any luxuries; he made up for it in ample measure with his love and care.

Lakshmi was born and Vaidehi followed within two years. Viswam and Rajam sensibly decided not to have any more children and lived wisely.

Rajam supplemented her household income by making poppadoms and chips. They lived a debt free and contented life; but that rainy day last year washed away all their happiness.

Finding it difficult to sell much, Viswam roamed a lot on the beach that evening, but gave up and decided to go back home.

As he walked along the main road in the pouring rain, carrying the snack tins, he couldn't spot a speeding car coming from the opposite direction and neither could the car driver see Viswam.

It was a disaster…

The driver used the rain to his advantage and fled the scene.

Viswam had lost both his legs, thigh down and suffered three fractures in his right hand. He lay in the general hospital for six months and Rajam suffered terribly, managing the children and the trips back and forth to the hospital.

Vedachalam came running on hearing about his son's accident. He expressed his grief and offered to help financially.

Viswam refused to speak to his father for a month; but how long could he continue to be stubborn and detached? After having spent months in poverty and desperation; Viswam realized that he could no longer afford to refuse the help his father offered and accepted everything without a word. Once Viswam was discharged from the hospital and returned home, Rajam found it extremely difficult to manage him, the two year old Vaidehi and five year old Lakshmi.

"Why should you suffer and struggle for two square meals? Why can't you come back home and stay with me? The little money that I have saved is for you, after all. Why are you so stubborn?" Vedachalam began to insist every time he visited them.

That evening, Rajam had just returned home exhausted after making murukkus at Saroja's place. She found Vedachalam sitting with Viswam. There were a few oranges, a couple of apples and a Horlicks bottle on Viswam's bed and the children sat with biscuit packets in their hands.

Once Vedachalam left, Viswam said, staring blankly at the ceiling, "For better or worse, he is my father; he is worried sick about me and I feel that we should be with him in his old age. Has he ever fought with us or did he drive us away? No, then why should we be so obstinate? With my condition being the way it is; living together with him will be most convenient for everyone. I am not able to see my father suffer and pine like this. He told me, he will come here with a vehicle tomorrow. I have made up my mind to go, do you hear me?"

Rajam realized that Viswam had come to this decision because he couldn't see her struggle endlessly and also because he would get a comfortable place to rest and get some nutritious food, at his father's place.

They were back at her father in law's place the very next day.

Vedachalam just kept to himself for the first few days and Rajam was very relieved. She wondered if it was because years had passed; she had become older, and had children, or because he was devastated due to what had happened to his son.

Whatever the real reason may have been; her relief proved to be short-lived and Vedachalam was back to his lecherous ways. He started with his usual tricks like, touching her, peeping at her on the sly and patting her. She was in a quandary. She couldn't tell anything to her husband, who had found peace after a long time.

Vedachalam became more and more brazen seeing Rajam's silence.

It was a Friday and Rajam woke up early, had her bath, and stood praying with her eyes shut. She suddenly opened her eyes, feeling some movement behind her.

It was Vedachalam.

He stood with a string of jasmine flowers in his hands. As she extended her hands to accept the flowers, he suddenly grabbed her and forcefully kissed her on her lips. Rajam was flabbergasted!

"You are like my father... Don't.... Appa... let me go..." She pleaded softly, pulled herself away from him, and ran into the kitchen.

That afternoon, as she sat with her head resting on Viswam's chest, she said sobbing softly, "Let's go back to living separately. I am scared of living here... please don't ask me the reason...Let's leave please."

Viswam listened to her in silence, and after thinking for a few moments, said with annoyance,

"Why are you creating such a scene? Nothing serious has happened! You know, I have become useless and it is Appa who is taking care of all of us like the man of the house. He too is human after all, isn't he? What is the problem with you? Why can't you do as he says?"

It was as if someone had poured burning coals on her. Rajam looked up at her husband with a start. Good food and a comfortable life had become his top priority. Viswam had realized that Rajam and he would not be able to afford these comforts however hard they worked in life.

So?

Is this selfishness? Is this the reason why he had spoken those heartless and insensitive words?

She stared at Viswam blankly as he flopped down on the bed tiredly. Rajam didn't say a word.

But, that Friday night, Rajam hanged herself with her saree and died.

1978

Biriyani

Natarajan stood on the verandah of his studio leaning on the parapet looking out at the street below.

He had had an unusually busy day since morning with back to back clients. The previous day must have been an auspicious one. There had been a steady stream of customers. Three newlywed couples, a group of college girls, a bare bodied baby… all wanting to be clicked from different angles!

Though Natarajan had opened his studio as usual at ten o'clock in the morning, he hardly had any time to have his lunch. He got a break only now at five in the evening. He had come out to the verandah, lit a cigarette and stood leaning on the wall, looking down at the street

This town was not Natarajan's hometown. He had been born and brought up in a village twenty miles away from this town.

His father was a farmer. Natarajan was the only son and he had two sisters.

Having failed the school final exams twice in a row, he lost even the little interest he had in studies and dropped all ideas of studying further.

"Join me in farming," said his father.

Natarajan didn't want to do that either. He had always been extremely fascinated by cinema; almost to the extent of craziness. One fine day, Natarajan just ran away to Chennai with two hundred rupees in his pocket, without informing anyone.

He somehow managed to get into a studio with the help of a friend and did odd jobs for ten years and even indulged in some objectionable activities before reaching the respectable post of an assistant cameraman. By the time Natarajan was twenty six years old he had picked up every possible vice and had faced every conceivable, unwanted, and unpleasant experience.

Once he had reasonable savings, he gathered the courage to visit his parents and landed at their doorstep in a taxi one fine day, dressed in a silk kurta, dhoti, and dark glasses. His mother, who had all along believed that her son was dead, was elated to see him.

"Your sisters are both married and well settled with their children and husbands. Appa has become old and is unable to take care of the land. Even I have become weak. Why don't you come back here and take care of the property and us?" His mother pleaded tearfully. God knows what power his mother's tears had; Natarajan could not focus on his old job once he went back to Chennai.

Natarajan was confused. It was true that he would enjoy the reputation of being a land-owner and have the comforts; but it was unimaginable for him to live in the village permanently.

What should I do? He wondered.

He thought deeply and decided to open a photo studio in the town twenty miles away using his prior work experience.

Natarajan did just that.

He set up the photo studio using the five thousand rupees Amma gave him plus his own savings.

He took the first floor of a building on one of the busy streets in town on rent. The place had two large rooms.

The one in front was his reception area cum office in the day time and his bedroom at night. The room at the rear was his studio. The small room adjacent to it worked as his dark room. He hung a colorful signboard which said 'Annai photo studio' in bold letters. His business picked up soon enough.

He would go to the village every Saturday night and return to town on Monday morning. He lived in the studio itself over the week. All his other activities too took place in the studio.

Natarajan felt amused every time his mother asked him when he was going to bring her a daughter in law and was reminded of a statement his friend from the cinema world had made. He had said, "Why should you bother buying a cow when you get ready fresh milk outside?"

The cigarette end scalded his hand; Natarajan jerked his fingers, throwing the butt away. He raised both his hands up and stretched himself. His eyes suddenly fell on the adjacent house where a young woman crouched on the floor was drawing a beautiful kolam.

Oh! The way her hips moved! The suppleness of that youthful body!

Natarajan was blown away!

Who was this woman? He didn't remember seeing her before.

His curiosity knew no bounds... he called out to Ganesan, his eighteen year old assistant, who was busy dusting the camera.

"Ganesa, who is that?"

"Who?" Ganesa came close to the parapet and asked looking down.

"Oh, that one…? She is their new maid. She has started coming for work only from Saturday."

Natarajan had gone to his village on Saturday to supervise the new sowing season and had probably missed seeing her.

"Is she easily accessible?"

Ganesan had worked as a light boy with Natarajan in the film studio in Chennai and he was a well-trained technician. He had been a constant support for Natarajan ever since he had opened this photo studio.

"I have no idea… I don't usually talk to those people." Ganesan replied.

Natarajan turned around and looked at her once more.

"Can you arrange to bring her here this evening?"

Ganesan nodded in response and walked back inside.

The two didn't need words to communicate with each other. Simple gestures were enough.

It must be 8 O'clock at night and the studio had been shut for the day. The streets had begun to calm down and the crowds had started thinning.

Natarajan sat on the sofa in the front office room checking the day's accounts when he heard approaching footsteps.

Ganesan, who had gone out at seven had returned; and behind him was that girl!

Ganesan beckoned to her saying, "Don't be afraid… come in."

"I have explained everything to her." He said and spread the fingers of his hands indicating 'ten rupees' towards Natarajan.

That's not much… thought Natarajan.

She stood hesitantly in one corner.

"Sit down," Natarajan said, gesturing towards her.

"It's alright."

Is she new to this?

Heavy silence pervaded the room for a few minutes.

"Will you have something to eat?"

She looked up with a glint in her eyes."

Natarajan realized that she was hungry.

"What do you want to eat?"

"……"

"Tell me… don't feel shy."

She whispered hesitatingly… "Biryani." Natarajan handed Ganesan some money and sent him to buy two packets of biryani and some strands of jasmine flowers.

Once Ganesan left, Natarajan asked, "Why don't you sit down? He has left."

She sat down.

"What is your name?"

"Mallika"

Natarajan looked at her closely and found her quite attractive. She was young; must be hardly twenty years old. She exuded freshness and vitality. She had changed into a different saree- one slightly better than the saree she wore in the morning. Her hands, legs and fingers were firm and beautiful owing to all the housework she did. But Natarajan found the dirt on her body and her grimy hair distasteful.

"Why don't you go and have a bath in the bathroom inside? There is soap and water kept ready."

She nodded and walked in gingerly.

Ten minutes must have passed; Ganesan returned with the food and flowers.

Natarajan gestured him to leave, asking him to come back later.

Natarajan opened the packet of flowers and smelt them. He placed the biryani packets on the table.

Mallika came out a few minutes later.

She looked clean and scrubbed; her sensuality heightened by the refreshing fragrance of soap.

"Sit down."

"Did you have your bath?"

"Yes."

"Will you have some biryani?"

"Yes."

He handed one of the biryani packets to her.

Mallika opened the packet and ate two mouthfuls and then asked, pointing at the other packet, "Is that also for me?"

She must be famished, poor girl!

"Yes, you can have it." Natarajan said, handing her the second packet.

Mallika opened the second packet and added the remaining biryani from the first one and packed it neatly.

She turned towards Natarajan and said, 'please let me go soon… the biryani is getting cold."

Natarajan was perplexed... what was the connection between him letting her go and the biryani getting cold?

"Why? Aren't you hungry? Do you want to eat it later? Why are you in such a hurry? You seem to be new..." Natarajan said sheepishly, sliding towards Mallika, and hugged her.

The touch of her cold body felt soothing.

He suddenly felt Mallika stiffen.

"Are you feeling scared Mallika? There is nothing to fear..." He said trying to make her feel comfortable. He then asked, attempting to put her at ease, "Where are you from? Are you from this town?"

Mallika sat with her head bowed and spoke softly...

"I come from a small village near Thiruvannamalai. I got married two years ago and my husband is a gem of a man... He had been working and earning well and I lived a charmed life. We were very happy and comfortable. Fate has been very cruel. Last year he suddenly suffered a stroke. He has become an invalid and that has led us to difficult times and a lot of suffering. Since he is now incapacitated, I have to work to earn a living. It has been a month since we came to this town for his treatment and also to look for work.. The meager amount I earn by working as a house maid is hardly enough to pay for his medical bills and I am not able to feed him a decent, hot, satisfying meal these days." She paused and tried to suppress a sob.

"That is why I agreed when your man approached me. My husband loves mutton biryani, especially when it is hot! Please...please can you send me quickly... so that I can serve him this biryani before it gets cold? Please?"

Seeing her eyes glistening with tears as she looked at him pitifully, Natarajan's grip around Mallika dropped and a strange, inexplicable sadness and helplessness engulfed him.

1977

Motherhood

She sat at the desk in her consultation room that was inaugurated just three days ago. It was a ten-by-fifteen room with a table and chair on one side and four metal chairs on the other. It had a long bench for checking patients, hidden by a Bombay dyeing curtain. There was a porcelain basin close to the table with water mixed with Dettol, a hand towel and a bar of lifebuoy soap.

This setup was enough for now she thought. She consoled herself saying she could always rent a bigger place once the patients increase. The only thing she missed having was a ceiling fan. She had a bad time sitting there from six to eight O'clock in the evening in the heat of the summer in June.

Even if she did decide to buy a fan without thinking about the expense, there was no hook on the ceiling. She thought of getting two holes drilled into the walls on both sides and fixing a metal rod to fix the fan, but a new ceiling fan would cost quite a lot and a good second hand one would be hard to find in this small town. She was also afraid that the dealers of second hand goods might cheat her by palming off some second-rate stuff because she was young and new in town. Moreover, she would have to run around looking for a mason and electrician. The senior doctor would surely help her if she approached him but how many times could she trouble him? In fact, he was the one who had suggested that she could do some consultations in the evenings and also helped her find this room in the marketplace. How could she seek more help from him?

She thought of having a table fan; but she had only one that she used at home. It would be difficult for her to lug it back and forth from the clinic to her house every evening, in case she decided to use the same fan in her clinic. Why not buy a new one? However, the price that the trader quoted had shocked her out of her wits. It was costlier than Chennai! She could easily buy a ceiling fan for that price. At least the ceiling fan would prove useful for patients as well. She felt that a table fan had other disadvantages; she would have to place it on a stool. The plug point was behind the door and she couldn't place the fan close to the door because it would be a hindrance for the patients. If she placed it on this side, where would the basin go? Finally, after thinking about all the alternatives, she decided to manage without a fan.

It was already June. The July breeze would start in a month's time and surely bring down the humidity.

It was hardly two months since she had moved to that small town. She had just completed her senior house surgery and was happily staying with her parents and working at the general hospital when she was suddenly posted to this small town as a junior doctor.

Hers was a government job; there was no way she could refuse to relocate.

She landed there and instantly hated the gloomy, run down hospital and the depressing town. It was very different from Chennai and her experiences here had been quite funny. Initially, she was astonished to see the village folk, their simplicity, and ignorance, but soon the same became annoying. She had to repeat every instruction at least four times.

Even after explaining to them clearly about the dosage and when to take the medicines, they would come back to her with the medicines the compounder gave them and bombard her with their doubts and questions.

"When should I have the blue capsules? Last time the senior doctor had given me yellow capsules. Don't you have them?"

"Give me an injection. I don't want tablets."

"Where is the senior doctor? You seem to be a novice. I want to see only him."

She began losing her patience and started shouting at her patients for no reason. The senior doctor called her and said, "I understand your feelings. This place is not like the city. These people are different and we need to have tremendous patience while dealing with these illiterate villagers."

She didn't say a word in response.

"Please don't think I am finding fault with you… this is my friendly advice. Once we come to work in such small towns; we need to develop a lot of tolerance. If someone sends a petition to the DMO, it will be a big hassle. Moreover, do you know that the people of this town are famous for sending petitions and anonymous letters for the most frivolous issues?"

She heeded his advice and tried to become more patient. She controlled her anger with a lot of effort and behaved cordially. It was quite difficult initially but she soon got used to it.

She stayed alone in a small portion of a house close to the hospital. She had a stout little 'man Friday' named Vairam who bought meals for her from the hotel, swept, and swabbed her portion, brought water for her bath from the well, and slept in the verandah at nights for security.

She was busy in the hospital from early morning till around eleven O'clock. She would come back home for lunch and rest till three thirty in the afternoon. She would then go back to the hospital for the evening shift and work till five thirty in the evening. Once she was back home, she would either read or go to watch some old movies in one of the three tent- theaters in town.

Somehow, she gradually managed to create a name for herself and gain the reputation of being a good doctor. The senior doctor appreciated her for her efforts and suggested, "Why are you getting bored in the evenings not knowing what to do? Why don't you open a small consultation room and have your own practice?"

The senior has settled in well in the place and has grown roots in the last three years. He has a comfortable house, earns handsomely with his private practice, and lives happily with his wife and children.

It was three days since she had opened her consultation room on the senior's advice. On the first day her only earning consisted of the five rupees her senior and another acquaintance gave her as a blessing for her private practice. On the second day, a girl paid her two rupees for an injection. Yesterday she had drawn a blank and the only people who came were those who wanted free treatment. God Knows how today would be!

She sat on the chair and looked at the clock. It showed 7.30. She decided to wait for another fifteen minutes and close the room if no patients showed up. It would be better to return home, have an early dinner, and hit the bed.

She still hadn't replied to her mother's letter that she received yesterday. Her youngest brother has been suffering from a bad cold and her mother had enquired about the medicines to be given to him. She decided to write her reply and searched her bag for an inland letter but couldn't find one.

She straightened the table cloth. The pen tray and her small prescription pad were placed neatly in the center of the table. She mentally praised Vairam for his meticulous work.

She was extremely bored and let out a loud yawn. She felt sticky because of the humidity and felt like having a cold water bath. As she decided to leave, she heard a loud voice, "Boy, is doctor madam there?"

As the woman walked into the room an unbearable stench spread all over. She must be around thirty years old. She stood with her disheveled hair, dirty saree, bloodshot eyes and swollen face. The woman seemed to be four months pregnant. The high fever had ravaged her body and she struggled to even stand properly. She spoke feebly, her mouth twisting,

"Are you the doctor? You look very young!"

She gestured towards the woman to sit down. The woman managed to sit with a lot of difficulty.

"What is the problem?"

"I have a high fever… I feel faint… give me an injection. I will be alright."

She checked the woman's pulse without saying a word, checked her chest and back with her stethoscope and asked the woman to show her tongue. She checked the woman's eyes. She made the woman lie down on the bench and closed the curtain.

"You know you are pregnant, don't you? I am going to check how many months it is. Just lie down still." She said wearing her gloves.

"What? Do you think you are a big doctor? You are not telling me anything that I don't know already. I don't want to know anything. Just give me the injection." The woman said agitatedly.

The woman tried to get up but she forced her to lie down saying, "It is wrong for me to give you any medicine without checking you. Just lie down quietly…"

She spread the woman's legs wide and as she bent down to insert her hands, the stench that rose from between the legs was unbearable.

Why is this woman stinking so much? Is it some kind of injury or infection? Why is the smell so rotten? She was shell shocked at what she saw!

She looked up at the woman and scolded her, "Do you realize what you have done?"

"What big mistake have I made? I just went to the self-proclaimed, untrained midwife and got the medicinal stick inserted; that is all! Usually, everything gets alright within two days, but this time it hasn't healed even after four days and the pain is unbearable. The fever is also high and that is why I came to you… give me the injection and I will be fine."

She was shocked to see the nonchalant attitude of the woman.

She had heard of innumerable crude methods the villagers used to get rid of unwanted pregnancies like getting sharp sticks from medicinal plants inserted into the womb to dislodge the fetus, using chili peppers or chemicals like Alum or abdominal massages with hot oils and herbs, but this was the first such case that she had to deal with and she was filled with disgust. It is relatively easy to abort a fetus within the first forty or fifty days but was it even possible to kill a fetus that was three months old by inserting a stick? What a horror! This woman must have suffered such unbearable pain in the last four days! What kind of a woman was she? There was no doubt that the baby had died but it hadn't come out fully and had begun to rot inside the womb. That must be the reason for the terrible stench. How was the woman tolerating the pain of the injury caused by the stick, the agony of the dead fetus stuck inside and the disgusting smell?

She felt very sad.

She made the woman sit close to her.

"What is your name?"

"Mariamma... Mari"

Ok Mari, what is your husband's name?"

Mari refused to give any further details.

"I can go to any bloody useless midwife and get the stick inserted. What is your problem? How does my husband's name matter to you? Just give me an injection for the pain and fever…stop bugging me with your questions. Tell me, will you give me the injection or not? Otherwise I will go to some other doctor."

She didn't like Mari's arrogance one bit but being a doctor she decided to control her anger and focus on treating the woman.

"You need to be treated immediately. It will be good to do a D&C. Come, let us go to the hospital."

"Hospital? No… do whatever you want here itself."

"That is not possible. I need sterilized instruments. Aren't you worried about your own life?"

"What can happen to me? Just give me the medicine and the injection. There is no need to go to the hospital."

Listening to the woman's refusal, she began to lose her patience. She retorted in an irritated tone,

"Do you know more about the problem or I do? The fetus is rotting inside your womb. If you are not treated immediately, it can be dangerous for your life. Why don't you understand? I will not give you the injection. You go to any doctor you want. Go!"

Her anger and strict tone made Mari afraid and she sat thinking silently for a few moments.

"Will I die if I don't come to the hospital for treatment? Really?"

"Yes."

"Will the hospital be crowded now? Will the shops around the hospital be open at this time?" The woman asked hesitatingly.

'Is this woman mad? She is talking nonsense!' She thought, but pacified the woman saying that it was eight O'clock and all the patients would have gone to sleep and the shops would have closed. Mari finally relented and agreed to come to the hospital with her.

She instructed Vairam to lock the consultation room, buy dinner, and go home. She went to the hospital with Mari in a cycle rickshaw. It was well past nine O'clock by the time she cleaned up Mari with the aid of a nurse on night duty, gave her medicine for the fever, an injection, and shifted her to one of the vacant beds in the casualty ward.

As she came home, showered and had her dinner in a daze, she also felt an immense sense of satisfaction of having saved someone's life.

Why hadn't Mari answered my questions properly? Had she tried to get the fetus aborted without telling her husband? Why did she say that normally she is fine in two days, but this time…? Does it mean that Mari had undergone other abortions as well? Did her husband know? Is she afraid that he will be angry if he came to know of the truth? Maybe she already has four or five children, and didn't want to have any more? Poor thing! It was so pathetic to see her pain and trauma! It would be so difficult for a mother to lose her child? Why was the poor woman afraid of coming to the hospital? Why was her attitude so nonchalant?

She couldn't sleep properly with all these questions raging in her mind. She woke up earlier than usual the next morning and went to the hospital. The ayahs and the nurses were busy cleaning the rooms and sponging the patients. As she entered her cabin next to the casualty ward, her eyes fell on Mari standing close to her bed with the support of an ayah. She could clearly hear what Mari was saying to the Ayah,

"I wanted to leave before daybreak, but couldn't. The man I am with right now owns the shop exactly on the opposite side of the hospital and there are chances that he will spot me because he is married and has also kept me as his mistress. I must leave before he sees me. I will be in trouble if he comes to know the truth…." Mari paused and then continued speaking, "Ayah, I will tie this cloth tightly around my stomach. You help me wear my saree over the cloth. I should look four months pregnant, do you understand?"

The one rupee that she gave the Ayah did the trick and Mari looked exactly how she did last evening.

"That man is shaken thinking that I am pregnant… He gives me money generously every time I ask him out of the fear that his wife will come to know the truth. Why should I bother? I have managed to get rid of this baby somehow… I will continue to go around with a cloth tied around my stomach for another six months and keep getting money from him. Anyway, it is no big deal… I will surely find another man after that, won't I…. I have to go… it is getting late Ayah…"

As she saw Mari wobble away slowly along the corridor, she was filled with an intense urge to kick Mari hard on her protruding stomach; and at the same time a wave of fatigue engulfed her.

1975

Vultures

The cry of the vultures was so loud and eerie that I found it hard to find the right words to express the experience.

They screech day and night! The damned creatures!

The sound became so loud that I got up from my desk and came to the window. There was a grove of Casuarina trees beyond the fields near my house. The vultures were among the birds that nestled there.

One of the vultures sitting on the oak tree spread its wings like an airplane and circled above my house and then perched itself on the fence. Suddenly, two more vultures took off and glided above screeching haughtily.

Why do they create such a ruckus? As I looked intently at the vulture sitting on the fence, I noticed that it was holding something round in its claws.

It was gray and fluffy.

The vulture on the fence ignored the other two vultures circling above and pecked hard at the fur ball in his claws with its sharp beak.

Once… and then again.

With the third peck, a long, red, string like thing came out.

Now I realized what that fur ball was. It was a dead rat which the vulture must have caught and was now blissfully eating it sitting on my fence.

I felt nauseous seeing the vulture grip the rat tightly between its sharp claws and tear open the dead animal's body with its beak.

No wonder they are called scavengers and birds of prey!

Why can't the stupid bird go elsewhere and eat?

I thought irritatedly.

I tried to shoo it away, but it didn't budge.

I couldn't take the screeching of the vultures circling above anymore. I closed the window and came back into my room.

"What should I cook for lunch today?"

I turned around listening to my cook's voice.

I was still disturbed by what I had seen just a while ago. I didn't feel like answering the old cook's question immediately.

"Since Sir is out of town, shall I cook some Sambar and curry?"

"Mm."

She walked away as I stood watching her. Her head was tonsured and she was draped in a white saree. She had a streak of sacred ash on her forehead.

The old cook must have been beautiful in her youth with her sharp nose and fair complexion.

She must be more than sixty five now.

Poor woman!

Working in someone's house to earn a living at this advanced age...

It was her misfortune and destiny...

Five years ago, I was looking for a cook when I received a letter from my aunt-Periamma from Tirunelveli in which she had written,

"There is an old woman here who is looking for a cook's job. She is a nice lady. Her family has gone through tough times. She is a fantastic cook. Shall I send her to your place?"

"Send her immediately." I replied and sent money for the lady's railway ticket.

The old woman arrived four days later.

I thought the woman would be around fifty years old from the way my aunt had described her. I was a little taken aback seeing that she was much older and frail.

"You look very old! Will you be able to do all the housework? We are used to eating on the dining table. You should not be too strict about following old traditions. You must bear with the children if they do mischief... Will it be possible for you, Patti?" I asked her bluntly.

Considering her age, I decided to call her Patti-grandmother.

She smiled a little and said, "I agreed to everything before I accepted to come here."

But we were in for a surprise.

Despite her age, Patti's work was impeccable. She cooked amazingly well and we were all very happy.

I had not asked her anything about her family yet. Periamma had hinted that they had gone through tough times. I didn't want to ask her something that could hurt her feelings.

I handed Patti her salary at the end of the first month.

"You don't give it to me. I will give you the address. Please send a money order."

She asked me to send the money to her son Ramu and requested me to write a few lines to him- "I am fine here. Take care of your health…. etc. the usual enquiries"

We got the receipt for the money order a few days later but there was no letter from her son.

"Why hasn't your son replied to your letter, Patti?"

"He may not have found the time. He has to cycle ten miles from Kallidakuruchi to go to school every day…"

Her son lived in Kallidakuruchi and worked as a teacher in a primary school in a nearby village.

Patti received a letter from her son on the thirty first of the next month. It said,

"I have developed a boil in my arm. Send five rupees more this month."

I sent five rupees extra on Patti's request.

It was a similar story the following month. This time it was a corn on his foot and he wanted ten rupees extra for treatment.

The five rupees advance of the previous month hadn't been deducted and now he wanted ten rupees more. What was happening?

"What is this Patti? Why is your son asking you to send money every month? Doesn't he get a salary? Why does a bachelor need so much money? When will I be able to adjust the advance if you keep sending him extra money every month?"

"Please send what he wants this month. You can start deducting from next month… poor fellow… he says he has corn on his foot. He gets one hundred and seventy five rupees a month. He has to pay rent, food and everything. It is difficult, you know…"

I wasn't convinced with her justification.

What kind of a son is he? Making his old mother to work and asking her for money…

I somehow didn't have a good impression of Ramu. It was the same story every month after that.

Have to prepare for exams; cycle repair; got stung by a scorpion; my salary got cut because of sick leave… there were all kinds of excuses each time.

He never enquired about his mother or acknowledged receiving the money she sent. He only wrote asking her to send more money each time.

Three months after Patti started working in our house; I couldn't take it anymore and asked her,

"What kind of a son is Ramu? Even if he doesn't take care of you; he can at least leave you alone and not trouble you! Why is he behaving like this?"

Patti, who sat cleaning the rice in the kitchen said, "I had ten children but unfortunately lost nine of them. He is the only one left. I will be at peace if he is well. At least I have a son to perform my last rites… Let him be happy wherever he is…"

Oh! So this is what it is! Is she pampering him because he is the only one alive?

"Did you have ten children Patti? What happened to the rest of them?"

Patti spoke grinding the rice,

"The first one was a daughter. She was beautiful. When she was about three years old, I had to go to my sister's daughter's wedding. My daughter was unwell, and my husband asked me not to go for the wedding but I insisted and went anyway. During the wedding ceremony, my daughter developed wheezing and those days we had no doctors or any medical facilities in our village.

I left for home before her condition deteriorated further. But by the time the bus turned around the corner, my daughter breathed her last. The people of the village refused to let me travel saying that a dead body cannot be taken out of town. I sat under a banyan tree with my child's dead body on my lap, not knowing what to do. My sister's mother in law sent me a spade and a shovel through someone, suggesting that I bury my daughter somewhere closeby. She was only worried about the wedding to go on as planned, her family prestige and well being. No one had the heart to think of my grief and distress. I buried my daughter like an orphan and returned home with my brother."

Pati's voice choked and tears welled up in her eyes.

Her second child, a son, died due to a tumor in his stomach. Her third daughter was kidnapped by someone for her gold jewelry. The kidnapper removed the jewelry the child was wearing and cruelly wrung her neck and threw her body into a well. Patti and her family found her daughter's bloated body after searching around for two days.

She lost two more children… one as a premature baby and the other to severe illness.

Raja, her son born before Ramu, was a handsome and well built boy. He was extremely close to his mother and insisted that he would take care of her like a queen once he grew up. But fate had different plans.

He got married when he was twenty three and suffered from Typhoid a year later.

It proved fatal and he fell silent forever.

Patti's tears streamed down her cheeks.

She was left with this lone, useless son, Ramu.

I couldn't believe Patti's story. How could a woman go through so much grief and continuous suffering? Is it even possible? Is it that she wanted to gain my sympathy and is cooking up such sob stories? I wondered.

But all my apprehensions were laid to rest within a few days.

Periamma from Thirunelveli had come to Madras for a wedding and visited us. She asked me while we were coming home from the railway station, "Is Patti doing well?"

"Oh yes, " I said nodding. "Patti is a nice person, but why is her son like this, Periamma?"

Periamma said, heaving a deep sigh,

"You should have seen the kind of life Patti lived those days. She was decked in gold jewelry... Pearl bangles on her wrists, gold earrings. She always wore heavy silk sarees with gold borders. Her husband was a lawyer and earned handsomely. His siblings cheated them and blew all the wealth away. She kept quiet all her life and suffered silently. Such a tragedy! She had ten children but lost one to wheezing, another to a stomach tumor. She lost nine children, her husband and all her wealth and is living a life of poverty and misery."

Oh! so everything Patti said was true! I was moved to tears.

Periamma whispered softly, "It is her misfortune that all her good children are gone and only this vagabond has survived. He is living with a woman from another caste and is the laughing stock of the town. Patti knows everything. But what can she do? You don't ask her anything. She is a very self respecting woman."

It was now clear why her son was constantly asking for money. The money the old woman was earning was going to her son's mistress!

What kind of a son was he?

Two years after Patti came to our house, I asked her, "Do you want to go and see your son? I will give you paid leave? Why don't you make a trip, Patti?"

"No. I may not be able to take the strain of traveling. It's enough that I know from his letters that he is well."

Now that I was aware of Patti's son, Ramu's character, I increased her salary by ten rupees and instead of giving it to her, I kept all the money with me. I explained to her saying, "Patti, if your son comes to know, he will ask you to send more. Let your salary be safe with me."

"Poor fellow, he too has expenses; he has to pay rent, and monthly chit funds. How will he manage? What am I going to do with all these savings? I just wish that he performs my last rite when I die… that is all I ask for." She repeated as usual.

With this Diwali, it would be six years since she came to my place.

I was woken up this morning by the loud screeching of vultures. Why should they create such a cacophony for no reason? I got up annoyed and looked at the clock. It was five in the morning. I decided that it was impossible to sleep anymore with all the noise and got out of bed.

I brushed my teeth and went into the kitchen.

Usually Patti would wake up at four, light the lamp in the pooja room, make the coffee decoction and go for her bath. I was taken aback to see the kitchen steeped in darkness. The lamp wasn't lit.

"Patti!"

What could be the reason?

I switched on the light and looked at Patti. I was shocked!

I called out to my husband nervously.

Patti had died peacefully in her sleep.

Nothing could be done.

I booked an urgent call to my Periamma and informed her about Patti's death,

"Please pass on the news to Patti's son and ask him to come immediately."

Periamma called an hour later and said,

"I went to their house but her son was not at home. His mistress was there. I gave her the news but she didn't even respond properly. She just said rudely, 'so the old woman has kicked the bucket, is it?' and walked away. Patti's son will come once he gets the news."

The day passed by and we got no response till evening. We finally received a telegram which said,"

"I am feeling unwell. Cannot come now. You go ahead and perform all the rites- Ramu."

The woman who had only one wish- that her only son should perform her last rites, had died an orphan's death.

The son, for whom she worked hard even in her old age had forsaken her!

My husband was upset and furious. He just thought for a moment and came to a decision.

He called a few neighbors and went ahead with all the preparations.

"I have had food cooked by her for so many years. She has fed me for so long. I too am like a son to her. Hence, I will perform her last rites." He said and they took Patti on her final journey.

I stood there contemplating.

At last Patti had found a gem of a son in my husband in her last moments. She was blessed indeed!

But Ramu? My blood boiled at the very mention of his name.

Was he a son?

Was he even human?

I could hear the screeching of the vultures in the background.

A thought crossed my mind suddenly.

These vultures were scavengers and fed on the carcasses of dead animals while Ramu had preyed on his mother's body bit by bit while she was alive!

He was worse than a horrible vulture. He had abandoned his mother the moment she died.

I heard the continued screeching of the vultures in the backyard but now it didn't bother me.

1975

Determination

The man who usually buys beef for Shyama didn't turn up that day. He took off saying they are harvesting sugarcane in the village.

Our house is situated in a factory premise on the highway, a kilometer away from the town. And we have to go to the town to buy all our daily needs.

Everyone close to me is aware that I have not brought up Shyama as a pet dog, but as my own daughter. When Shyama was a little pup, the veterinary doctor had told me, "Alsatian dogs have weak hind legs and they need to be fed beef to keep them strong." I have followed his instructions and have been feeding beef regularly.

We have a person assigned to get the beef from town.

I have separate vessels, a gas stove etc. in the backyard to cook the beef

Whenever my friends praise Shyama saying, "She has grown so strong and healthy!" I start singing my usual tune, "Oh! Thank you! But it's not a joke… I feed her one kilo of beef… no rice for her. I cook the beef separately. She loves it!"

Whenever I visit anyone's house and find their dog weak or thin, I start giving them unsolicited advice, "Why is your dog so thin? Why don't you feed her beef? Try it and see how healthy your dog will become. Even my Shyama…" I go on and on endlessly.

The man who usually bought the beef had not come. What could I do?

I called the driver and asked,

"Do you know where they sell beef in town?" He nodded a 'yes'.

"Alright, get the car. I have some work in town. We will also buy the beef for Shyama."

"Aiyo! You don't go to such places Amma."

"Why?"

"You will not like those places." He said hesitatingly.

I laughed aloud, "I was a Zoology student in college and have dissected frogs, rabbits, and sharks, and I am not disgusted by all this. Let's go."

We reached the highway and after crossing three quarters of the town, we turned into a gravelly road towards the left. There was a pond a hundred meters ahead. The water was green. I wasn't sure if it was because of moss or something else. After we crossed the pond, we came to a small building on an elevation. We could see rows of meat hanging through its doors and windows.

The driver stopped the car about twenty feet before the building. A nasty stench hit us as we stepped out of the car.

I handed the money for the beef to the driver and asked him to return fast.

There was a big slum on the other side of the road. Seven or eight children came running and surrounded our car.

All of them were bare bodied except for their loin cloths.

They were all grimy and their hair was disheveled and dirty. Some of the younger boys had running noses while some of the others had red bruises on their noses due to constant cold. One of the boys who peeped into the car through the open window shouted excitedly, "hey, this car has a radio!"

All the boys milled around the car and looked at me as if I was an alien. One of the boys drew a straight horizontal line on the side of the car with his stick.

"You boys, move away," The driver shouted as he walked back. The vessel in his hand was empty.

"They have just butchered the animal Amma. There are a lot of people waiting inside. It will take some time for them to cut pieces."

The boys scurried away seeing the driver and jumped gleefully into the moss ridden pond, one after another.

"Ah, It is cold."

"Ye!!"

"You also come."

They all seemed to be having a good time, spitting out mouthfuls of the dirty water and splashing around. Suddenly, I spotted something bloated like a balloon floating close to the boys.

"What is that?" I asked the driver.

"It is the skin of the cow butchered in the morning."

I felt a wave of sympathy and sadness seeing that scene. As I sat watching, a man with a red towel wrapped around his waist came out of the building. He had a knife-like thing in one hand and a pinkish skin in the other. He got into the pond and rubbed the cow skin on a rock lying nearby. A red and white fluid drained into the pond.

The same nasty stench rose yet again.

I felt queasy and discomfited.

"Hey, hey!"

I turned towards the voice.

A man with a towel tied around his head, came to the building, pulling an emaciated and skinny cow.

He tied the cow near the building and walked in.

"I think they will butcher one more cow because there is a lot of crowd today." The driver said without waiting for me to ask anything.

I was shocked.

"Will they butcher it here? Isn't there a separate place for that?"

"They may butcher it here. That is why I had asked you not to come, Amma."

As if to prove him right, the man who walked in, came out carrying an iron pestle and a broad knife.

I began to tremble.

I rushed out of the car and said to the man pleadingly, "please… don't butcher the cow now… just wait for five minutes. I will leave soon." I turned to the driver and said hurriedly, "Go and get it fast. Even if they are big pieces, it is alright."

The driver could understand my state and he ran into the building.

I turned to look at the cow and man who had thankfully accepted my request,

It was a light brown cow. It was all skin and bones; and had a bridle pierced through its nose.

Its horns were freshly painted red and green for the Pongal festival that went by recently. In this harvest festival cattle are worshiped with great pomp and show.

The man, who was going to sell the cow for beef, had just worshiped it a few days ago! What an irony!

I wondered what the cow must be feeling seeing the pestle and knife in the man's hands. Would it have realized that it is going to die in the next few minutes?

Is it fear in those dark eyes? Why was its face so sullen? My sorrow deepened as I looked at it.

When they say, 'Patience like a cow', do they mean this?

Is this what patience means?

I couldn't take it anymore.

I pressed the car horn to remind the driver to hurry.

He came running.

The filthy, green pond and the children splashing around in it…

Their health and hygiene…

The helpless cow…

The man standing totally oblivious to everything around him…

All these disturbing images shook me. I got back into the car.

Oh God, when will our country improve?

The driver was unable to turn the car into the narrow lane and had to go almost hundred meters in reverse gear.

We must have gone hardly twenty feet.

I turned around and saw it happening.

I heard a heart-rending cry…

"M.. oo… oo….."

The man had waited for exactly five minutes and then done his job.

While another person held the horns of the cow, the man with the towel on his head hit the cow hard between its horns.

"M.. oo… oo….." The cow cried pitifully as its mouth frothed and its eyes popped out. The cow's legs twisted and it flopped down on the ground.

One more hit… and a third one…

Even as the cow's legs twitched, the other man took the knife and began cutting the cow's neck.

All this happened within the three or four minutes the car took to reach the main road in reverse gear.

I was numbed and dazed beyond words.

I couldn't take the shock of what I had seen and my sorrow knew no bounds. Tears streamed down my eyes.

"Amma, this is why I told you not to come". The driver said in an attempt to console me. I said nothing and we came home in silence.

I described everything to my husband and sobbed uncontrollably.

"They kill the animals so brutally! Should they torture them so badly? Can't they tranquilize the animals before they butcher them?" I screamed in rage.

"I have decided that I will not feed Shyama beef anymore. I will not buy the meat of cows tortured in such an inhuman manner. This is final." I said with determination.

My husband replied calmly, "Do you think the brutality will stop just because you decide to discontinue feeding Shyama beef? All you will do is ruin Shyama's diet…"

But I didn't change my mind. The next day, when the man who bought the beef regularly came for work, I sent him away saying I didn't need him anymore.

Shyama had been fed eggs and milk in the morning, but she sat in the backyard at two in the afternoon waiting to be fed again. I could hear the maid tell Shyama, "No beef for you, Go away."

I went into the kitchen and mixed a bowl full of rice and lentils with ghee and put it into Shyama's bowl. Shyama came running with anticipation and hunger. But she sniffed at the food, turned her face, and went back to the backyard where the beef is usually cooked.

I was livid.

"Let her be. She will eat this food when she is really hungry." I mumbled in anger.

Shyama refused to eat anything the whole day.

The next morning, when Shyama refused to have the milk, I was enraged.

"How stubborn can she be?" I thought but at the same time I felt pity for my beloved daughter; my heart melted seeing her starve herself.

Shyama became really uneasy by afternoon and lay listlessly in the backyard.

She barked for no reason and followed me around. Her eyes seemed to beg me saying, "Amma, I am hungry."

Shyama refused to touch milk, eggs, bread or fish oil.

Seeing her hungry, I also couldn't eat anything that evening and I skipped dinner.

It has already been two days since Shyama has eaten anything. She was weak but still stubborn.

Looking at her condition, I relented and called the driver.

"Do you know how they butcher goats? Is it similar to the way they butcher cows?" I asked.

"No Amma. It's a single cut in the case of goats."

I was a little relieved.

"OK! In that case go quickly and get mutton for one rupee."

"One rupee won't be enough Amma."

When he came back with two rupees worth of mutton, there were exactly eight pieces.

"What is this? This is so less!"

"Yes Amma, Mutton is ten rupees a kg… beef is only one rupee."

I was surprised. "Is there so much difference?"

Shyama was used to eating a bowlful of beef. This will surely not be enough for her.

The next morning I asked the driver to buy mutton for three rupees but that too proved inadequate. Shyama had lost a lot of weight within four days. I didn't know what to do and I just couldn't sleep that night.

Shyama continuously whined and moaned. I just couldn't take her constant pleading for food.

My husband left it to me saying, "It's between you and your daughter; leave me out of it." Everyone in the household was annoyed with my obstinacy that was causing Shyama so much trauma.

I thought a lot… Again and again…

I was reminded of how I used mosquito repellent sprays in the evenings to get rid of the menace. Didn't I feel elated seeing the mosquitos fall dead? Didn't I get vicarious pleasure out of seeing ants run helter-skelter? Didn't I kill living creatures for the sake of my own comfort?

Wasn't the butcher doing the same? He too was killing cows the way he knew, just to earn a living and take care of his family, wasn't he?

The more I thought I could sense my determination beginning to melt.

I looked at Shyama, 'Amma, why are you starving me for the sake of your own determination? You got me used to eating beef and now you yourself are depriving me of my favored diet. Is it my fault...?'

Is this what Shyama would be thinking?

My determination had vanished completely. I came to a decision finally.

That morning, I asked the servant to call the man who bought the beef for Shyama.

We all have heard the term 'smashana vairagyam' or the sense of detachment we feel when someone close to us dies and we go to the crematorium for the last rites. At that time, we resolve not to get attached to anything in life. But soon enough our determination wears away and we return to leading our normal lives with all our attachments coming back.

There is also something called 'prasava vairagyam' which is the detachment felt by a pregnant woman, when she is delivering her baby. The pain is so unbearable and severe; she resolves that she will never go through this ever again. But as soon as her son is born, and the pain is forgotten, she tells her husband that she wants to have a daughter. The determination vanishing as fast as it comes…

Which of the two categories does my determination fall into?

1974

— The End —

www.ingramcontent.com/pod-product-compliance
Lightning Source LLC
Chambersburg PA
CBHW051437130726
47987CB00005B/2083

9 789394 922389